Losing Control

Dedication:

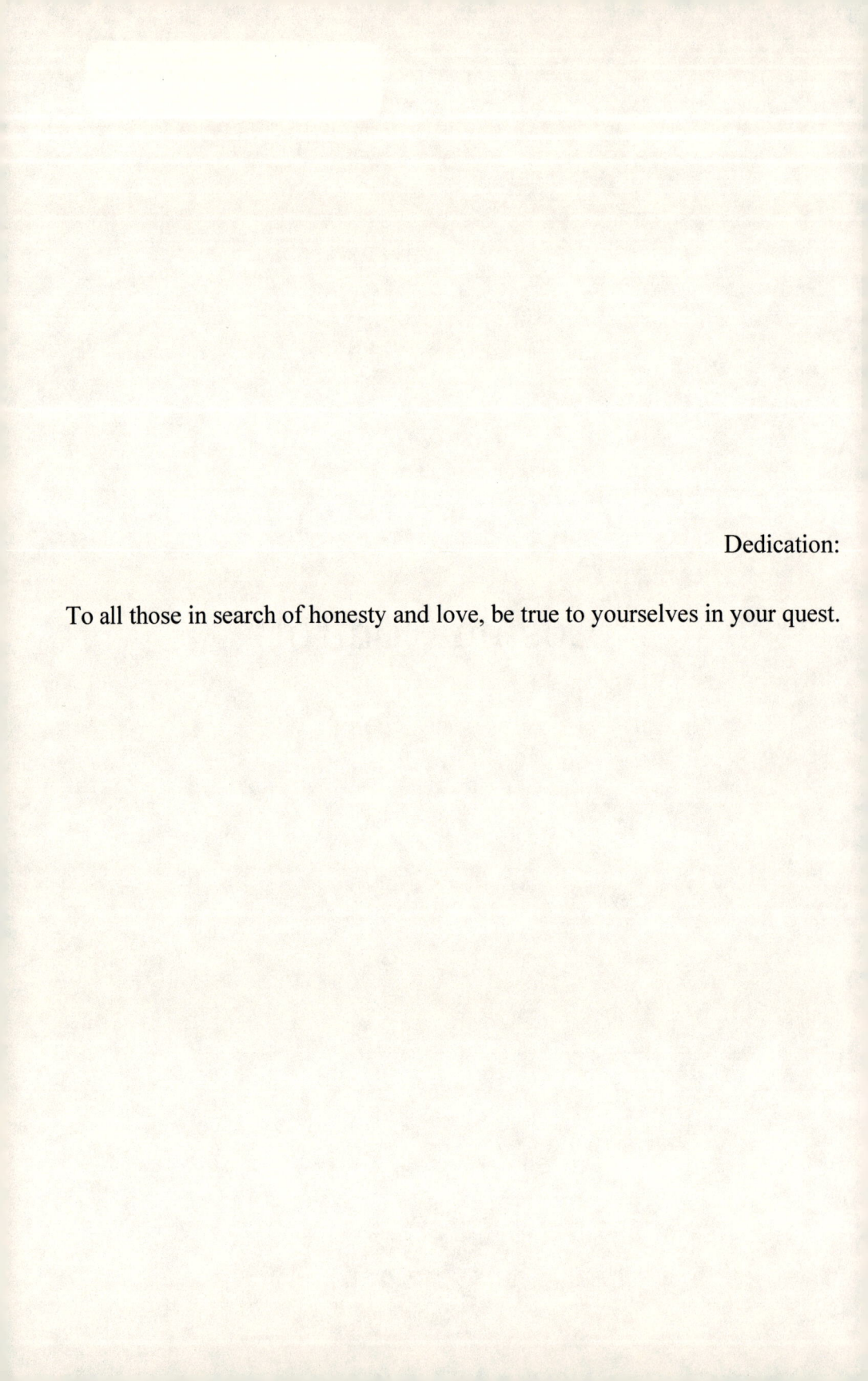

To all those in search of honesty and love, be true to yourselves in your quest.

This book is a work of fiction. Resemblance to persons, locations, or characters real or fictional, living or deceased is entirely coincidental and unintentional except where the author has written permission for such characterization.

Copyright ©2009 Cheril N. Clarke

Cover Design by: N'Digo Design

This book was published by Dodi Press, and printed in the United States of America in 2009. All rights reserved.

No part of this publication may be reproduced or transmitted in any form or by any means, electronic, mechanical, or digital, including photocopying, recording, or otherwise, or by any information storage and retrieval system without the prior written permission of the copyright holder. Requests for such permission should be addressed to: Dodi Press, PO Box 892, Mt. Laurel, NJ 08054

ISBN-10: 0-9767273-2-3

ISBN-13: 978-0-9-767273-2-3

Cheril N. Clarke

Losing Control

by Cheril N. Clarke

Losing Control

Chapter 1

Her eyes were closed but she was awake. Facing the wall with her back against his, she debated slipping out of bed but remained still. She didn't want to wake him, nor did she want to chance catching a glimpse of herself in one of her bedroom mirrors. Guilt and shame made her feel ugly. Her breathing was deliberately soft, almost undetectable before she took a weighted breath as if to relieve the pressure that had been building for so long. It was three o'clock in the morning and Brianna had barely slept an hour since she had lain down at eleven.

Opening her eyes, she stared at the clock on the nightstand, blinking, thinking. She turned to face him and kissed his smooth, dark brown shoulder. He sighed peacefully and reached for her arm to place it around him. A tear slid from her right eye onto the pillow. With her hand against his chest, she could feel his heartbeat. She could feel the warmth radiating from his athletic, 5'9" frame. Brianna inched closer to him so that her bare skin was against his, closed her eyes, and again tried to sleep. Lately, this had become a routine, although he had no idea. It was always in the middle of the night that her deepest feelings gnawed at her from within. She kept it all inside, as if telling someone about them would cost her everything she'd worked for. It might have.

Franklin and Brianna had become friends during their years at Rutgers University's School of Law and remained so after they had both graduated with honors. Although he had gone on to become a powerful businessman in Philadelphia, she had moved forward with her interest in local politics, using her law degree as padding for her already bulging résumé. Over the last six months, they'd become intimate, something they hadn't done since a one-time experience during their schooldays. Unable to stand the lonely nights in her home, Brianna occasionally invited Franklin to spend evenings with her. He was a strong, handsome, and incredibly intelligent man—a rarity, especially in comparison to the men whom she saw on a daily basis in the gritty southern city of Rockville, New Jersey. Franklin lived one town over in Cherry Hill, not very far away but starkly different with its shopping malls, trendy restaurants, and roomy homes on big lots of manicured lawns. He lived in a high-rise condominium. Brianna cared for him, but the way she'd been using him was wrong and she knew it.

As the night began to turn into early morning, she finally fell asleep. Their bodies were closely spooned together under soft, sea-green sheets. Two hours later Frank woke up and turned around to kiss her on the forehead before easing out of bed and into the bathroom to begin his morning routine.

"Bri," he lowered his tenor voice to a whisper after returning to her side and sitting on the edge of the bed.

"Hm?" She opened her eyes slowly to see a half-smile on his face. She managed to return one of her own.

"I'm about to head out." He ran his hand down her arm and, admiring her soft, medium-brown skin, took her hand in his. "I umm..." Franklin hesitated, unsure if he should say what he was thinking. He decided against it. "I'll call you later, okay?"

"All right."

He leaned in to kiss her again, softly grazing her bottom lip with his tongue before pulling away. She smiled, feeling a tingle in her body. Franklin's touch was somewhat comforting. She got up to walk him out and then crawled back into bed for a few more hours of shuteye.

Brianna scrolled through messages on her PDA as she waited in a drive-thru for her coffee. Thoughts of Franklin ran rampant in her mind, but she pushed them aside. Because of him, her personal and professional lives were merging. She felt terrible about it but knew she needed him if she was going to win the election. Franklin was connected to a lot of influential and well-off people. Now that she was running for city council, she had to tap every resource that she had.

After getting her coffee, she headed toward her storefront headquarters. Her cell phone soon rang.

"Good morning, Sheldon." She could see from the caller ID that it was her campaign manager.

"Morning, Anderson. I hope you're on your way in. You have a tight schedule today."

"I am. I am. I'll be there soon."

"Okay. Let me brief you really quickly anyway," said Sheldon.

"Go ahead."

"You have two 'Meet the Candidate' appearances with Smith."

"Ugh."

"I know you hate those, Anderson, but they're a must."

"Mm hm," she sighed. "Next?"

"A fundraising dinner," he paused, "and speaking of fundraising…"

"I know, dial-for-dollars." She didn't know which task she dreaded more: appearing with her opponent, Colleen Smith, or personally calling people to request donations to her campaign. "Sheldon, I'll be there in a few minutes, okay?"

"All right, I'll see you in a few then," he said and they hung up.

"I guess I'd rather ask for money than be next to Smith," she muttered to herself.

The last time Brianna had been in the presence of Smith, there had been an aura of disdain and jealousy emanating from her rival. After they were out of the public eye and Brianna had extended her hand to Smith, she was taken aback by her reserve. Smith walked out of the room without a word to Brianna, her silence coming off as snobbish and condescending. The closer it got to Election Day, the more tense things became.

Brianna thought she had a good chance of winning, but in reality, no one who was currently in office backed her because she was different—a young hotshot who, though a Democrat, had ideas that were more conservative than the current leadership in the crime-infested city. She wanted to take over the fifth district, a first step toward taking over the city. Rockville resonated deeply with Brianna because it reminded her of the shoddy East New York section of Brooklyn in which she had been born and raised. The eyes of the people were the same. The mix of despair, fatigue, and complacency within them made her think of the many days she had looked around East New York wanting to change things but being too young and ill-equipped to do so.

The day that she'd made up her mind to make a difference in a poverty-stricken neighborhood was a day during which she had barely escaped being hit by a stray bullet. It had killed an innocent child instead. Brianna never forgot the earsplitting sound of the fired shots and the scenes of chaos as people darted for cover. A burning desire to escape the trap of living in housing projects pushed Brianna to become as educated as possible. She had excelled and risen to become a force to be reckoned with. While pursuing her undergraduate degree, she had spent a semester working as an intern for New Jersey's Senator Buckley at the Capitol in Washington, D.C. It was there that she had taken a serious interest in New Jersey's local politics. Long before she had even moved to the state, she had begun learning about its cities and its people. Rockville caught her attention as a place where she could make a difference for the residents, as well as make a name for herself. Brianna Anderson, City Councilwoman; she said the title over and over in her head. She wanted it badly and would stop at nothing to obtain it.

Chapter 2

An audience of about twenty people sat inside the small community room of a senior citizens home. Four of them were asleep, two of them were staring out a window, and one man was digging in his ear. The rest were barely paying attention, but Colleen Smith went on with her speech anyway. It was her third stop of the day and she didn't seem a bit tired. Time felt as though it were going by quickly, and she was giving her campaign all she had.

Having won previous elections by wide margins, Colleen was now uncomfortable with Brianna's candidacy, but she tried to hide it. She didn't like the change that Brianna represented. Colleen was born and raised in Rockville. She'd seen it in good times and in bad. She could remember when it flourished, before blue collar work suffered a miserable death at the hands of a crippled economy. As factories closed one by one and work began to disappear, the city began to tumble into reckless neglect. But Colleen had lost her compassion for Rockville a long time ago. For the latter part of her career, she had been part of a small group of people who had a stronghold on the city. She was guilty of retaining her power through corrupt pay-to-play systems, accepting large contributions from professionals in return for awarding them no-bid contracts. She had a number of other tricks up her sleeve that help offset the meager salary of a councilwoman. Colleen only cared about herself.

"Listen, I want you to dig up some dirt on Brianna Anderson," she said to her campaign manager, Tony, after they left the senior citizens' home. She brushed her thin, dark brown hair from her face.

He looked at her without giving a response.

"I'm serious. I don't care how you do it, but find some dirt and leak it to the press!"

Tony restrained his impulse to talk with reason and nodded in acknowledgement. "Consider it done."

She placed her hand on his arm. "Don't let me down."

He relaxed. "I won't. I know a guy who can find anything on anyone. Just give me a little time."

"You've got it," she said and pointed her finger at him sternly, "but not too much time. I want this done."

He nodded positively. "Don't worry."

They soon were in the meeting room of a neighborhood association. The residents greeted Colleen warmly. *Smile, shake hands, compliment. Smile, shake hands, compliment.* Over and over, she went through the same motions with everyone after formally introducing herself. She worked the entire room; most of the people in attendance already favored her over Brianna. She was in one of the few sections of Rockville that wasn't downtrodden by violence and poverty, one where she'd recently gotten a state-of-the-art recreation center built for children. The residents loved her, willingly placing campaign signs in their lawns. *Smile, shake hands, compliment...pose for a picture and keep smiling.* Colleen was a hit.

In the Anderson headquarters, Brianna's eyes were fixed on the television. Breaking news: An entire family had been shot execution style in a row house that had been set on fire in an attempt to cover up the killings. A toddler and newborn were among the dead.

"Can the district look anymore unsafe?" She sighed and bit her bottom lip. "This is bad. This is awful timing."

"It's bad for the families, but only awful timing for you if you make it," Sheldon said. "You have a speech tomorrow morning before your fundraising luncheon. I'm going to tweak it to show compassion for the victims while reinforcing your stance that Rockville needs new leadership."

She ran her manicured hands through her hair while nodding in agreement. "I need to have that speech for review tonight."

"I'm on it right now."

"I appreciate you, Shel." Brianna flashed her dimple-accented smile.

"Don't worry about it," he said, before stepping away to work alone.

Brianna's cell phone vibrated. It was Franklin. She sent the call to voice mail, making a mental note to call him when she had privacy.

"Is Yesenia back yet?" Brianna asked the question aloud to no one in particular but waited for a response. Yesenia was a young, cute, Hispanic volunteer.

"I haven't seen her," answered Asad while typing rapidly.

"Thanks, Asad." Brianna smiled at him and quickly turned her attention to a wall that had a large district map taped to it. Next to the map was a sizeable calendar that had all of her important dates marked in red.

"Anderson." Sheldon called her.

"Yes?"

"I've made the revisions to your speech. Why don't you take a look?" His eyes were large and prideful as he handed her the pages. Sheldon was a smart man in his mid-fifties, short, balding and slightly overweight.

"All right, Shel. Just give me one minute." Brianna set the papers down and continued to scan the calendar.

Yesenia walked into the headquarters empty-handed with a grin on her face. She'd gone door-to-door to distribute literature about Brianna and to try to drum up more volunteers to help with a mass mailing that was coming up.

Brianna looked toward Yesenia. "I was just asking about you."

"Sorry, I stopped to grab something to eat on my way back." She smiled apologetically. "Did you need something?"

Losing Control

"I just wanted to know how it went for you today. Were people receptive and taking the literature or did you just end up leaving most of it on doors?"

"Well, some people took the info and said they'd read it later, a hand full of people asked me questions about you, and I did end up leaving some at houses where no one answered the door."

"Thank you so much."

"It's cool." Yesenia smiled.

Brianna returned her attention to the revised speech. After making a few minor changes, she gave it her stamp of approval.

The day passed quickly. She had a staff meeting with her team and then left for several meetings with ministers and civic organization leaders. She was also scheduled to have dinner with Terrence, a close friend of Franklin's. The two men had grown up together in Rockville and even pledged to the same fraternity in college. Together, and with some of their other frat brothers, they'd started an adopt-a-street program in an effort to clean up Rockville. The streets they had chosen happened to be in Brianna's voting district, and Terrence was leading the project.

Terrence had a personality that drew people to him. In addition to his adopt-a-street program, he owned a barbershop and was known for changing the lives of young men who were open to listening to his advice and guidance as well as that of his older, life-experienced barbers. Before becoming an entrepreneur, Terrence had been an investment banker in New York. He'd simply grown tired of Corporate America and had branched out on his own in a way that provided more meaning to his life. He tried to train and employ as many people as he could. He even employed kids to sweep up the shop when they were out of school, but they had to prove that they did actually go to school. Terrence wanted to give back to the community from which he had come.

At the restaurant, Brianna looked him directly in the eyes as she spoke. "Thanks so much for meeting with me tonight."

"It was my pleasure. I really think you can do some good in Rockville. I'm behind you one hundred percent. I'll do what I can to help."

The waiter interrupted. "Sir, madam, how was everything this evening?"

"Fine, thank you." Terrence and Brianna answered simultaneously.

"Would you care for dessert or coffee?" The waiter continued as he cleared the table.

"Actually, I'm fine. Thanks." Brianna answered and then looked at Terrence.

"Just the check," Terrence added. The ring that he wore on his pinky finger glistened as he reached for his glass of water.

The waiter left and returned quietly with the check as Brianna and Terrence wrapped up their conversation. Terrence was willing to donate $1500.00 to her campaign, call upon his friends to do the same, and post her signage in his shop. She studied his mannerisms, his polished, matter-of-fact way of speaking, and even noticed his Philadelphia Eagles personalized license plate when they walked to their cars. He was well dressed with a black jacket and a starched mint green button-down shirt tucked into black slacks that had razor sharp creases in them. His bald head suited his boyish good looks. She could see how he and Frank were good friends. They were similar in a lot of ways.

"Get home safely," he said after giving her a hug. She caught a drift of his cologne, masculine, but not too strong.

"And you do the same. I'll be in touch."

"Sounds good."

When Brianna finally decided to call it a night, she phoned Franklin while she was on her way home but he didn't answer. She tried again when she got to her condo but still got no answer. She brushed it off and placed her phone on its charger before deciding to pour a glass of wine. An hour of sipping her drink and reviewing her speech had passed before she decided to take a shower. Her house was quiet. Lonely.

Brianna had never been in a truly fulfilling relationship. She had come close to it once, however. *Sadira*. The name wafted through her mind plenty of times over the years although they hadn't spoken to each other. Sadira was the one who got away. After a few months of dating, Brianna had relocated to pursue her internship and vowed that for the sake of her career, she was no longer going to date women. She thought if she was going to make it in politics as a

Republican, which she was at the time, she had to conform to the mainstream. She didn't realize that her true political beliefs were aligned closer to center-Democrats than Republicans until her experience as an intern, which eventually led her to switch parties. Republican ideals sounded good in theory but when implemented, often proved to never be able to hold their own and offer trickle-down help to people who come from environments like the one from which she had come. She had also naively thought she could work around the religious drive of the party, but it was too difficult. Some of the people she had worked with unabashedly used Christianity to drive public policy, regardless of if it trampled people's freedom of religion. From viewpoints on marriage equality and aid to the poor, Brianna found herself disagreeing with her party as she matured. Things weren't as easy or black and white as Republicans made them seem. Immersed in her work, Brianna experienced a lot of political growth from that summer on. Her constant problem, however, was her lack of an ideal personal life. Though she acted as though she was content, she was not.

Besides Franklin, she wasn't intimate with anyone else. He was better than a vibrator and she did care for him, but she wanted… needed, and *craved* a woman. She wanted the emotional attachment that only a woman could give her. Every day her suppressed feelings made themselves more apparent as they fought to reach the surface. She began to wonder how long she could deny herself the connection she so badly needed.

After a long, hot shower, she changed into her black silk pajamas, climbed into bed under a thick comforter and turned off the lights.

"Mmm." Franklin's deep moan was a ballad in Yesenia's ears as he felt himself reaching a powerful climax.

"¡Sí, Papá, sí! Damelo!" Holding on to him tightly, Yesenia spoke in her native tongue as she too approached a sexual peak. It was her second escapade with him that evening. The stack of literature that she was supposed to distribute for Brianna was outside in the parking lot sitting on the passenger seat of her car.

"Frank…" Yesenia whispered his name as she lay beside him, pleasurably exhausted.

"Yeah?"

She used an index finger to trace the contours of his chest and abs. "That was so good. I could make love to you all day."

He laughed nervously and kissed her in response.

Guilt. Brianna crossed his mind after hearing Yesenia's statement. Even though he and Brianna weren't exclusive, he felt like he was betraying her. He tried to push her out of his mind to rid the heavy feeling. Eventually he and Yesenia fell asleep with their backs turned toward each other.

Franklin didn't know what he was doing with Yesenia. She was beautiful, but he didn't care about her. Deep down he was lonely. He wanted companionship, a partnership that Brianna was unable to give him. Sometimes he thought that being with the two of them would make up for what he wanted from one individual, but it wasn't working that way. He was unfulfilled and the only difference between Yesenia and Brianna was that he actually cared about Brianna. Their friendship had been firm for years, but he was skating on thin ice by sleeping with someone who was on her staff. Of all the people he could be with, he felt incredibly idiotic for getting into a physical relationship with someone who worked for Brianna. His stupidity haunted him and every day he woke up telling himself that he should break things off with Yesenia for the sake of his friendship with Brianna. He just never got around to doing it.

Chapter 3

The next morning, Brianna talked about the race and looked over her speech as she rode to a rally site with Sheldon. She was concerned that her name recognition wasn't what she wanted it to be at that point in her campaign.

"Don't worry," Sheldon told her repeatedly. He was ever confident that she would emerge triumphantly in the end. He had been watching her grow from unknown to known in just a month and knew that her feelings were attributable to first-time campaigning jitters.

"I'm okay." She lied. She had had a restless night and was actually very tired, but she didn't want it to show.

At their destination, Frank, Terrence and a few of their fraternity brothers were getting things in order for Brianna and the other invited guest speakers. She had about 15 minutes before she was due to address the crowd and took the time to look over her speech once again to memorize it as much as she could. She didn't like reading directly from the paper because it cut down on the time she could make eye contact with the audience.

"Okay, it's time." Sheldon patted her on the shoulder. "Knock em' dead, Anderson."

She smiled and straightened out her navy blue skirt suit. "I will." Wearing very light make-up, Brianna purposely played down her looks. She didn't want people to think she was all beauty and no brains, but she didn't want them to perceive her as was frumpy either. She always managed to find a proper balance.

The audience applauded after her introduction. "Thank you very much," she said and paused briefly to glance around the room. She took in its white walls and the empty white plastic chairs in the back. A slender man wearing a black shirt and gradient red tie sat up front along with a few women and a journalist who held a recorder in one hand and a notebook in the other. She was happy to get a good turn out on a Saturday morning.

"It is a pleasure and an honor to be with you all today. This morning, we're going to talk about change. We're going to discuss becoming politically mature and taking control of our city." She moved from behind the podium.

Two people walked in late.

"Now, I'm sure you all have heard about the horrific shooting and fire yesterday," Brianna continued.

"Terrible, just terrible. We shouldn't have to live like this!" Someone from the audience added her own comments.

"Yep!" Another person in the audience responded immediately. Murmurs and whispers began to fill the room but quieted when Brianna started speaking again.

"I know," Brianna responded. "I watched the news just like you. And I live in Rockville just like you. We're facing very serious problems. Problems that the current leadership has done nothing to help alleviate. Sure we've heard about agendas and initiatives, but I have yet to see results."

People in the audience began to lean forward in their chairs.

"The truth is Rockville doesn't need another band-aid, more government aid, or leaders masquerading as saviors of the poor when they really only care about themselves." She paused. "Rockville needs a change in leadership, a change in its direction. It needs its pride restored and jobs created so that the people who live here can have a sense of dignity. An increase in jobs will equal a decrease in crime!"

"That's right!" someone in the audience yelled.

"Together we can make the changes we need, changes that will lead us into a better future."

People nodded in agreement and applauded. She noticed a woman in the back of the room whose face was familiar, but she couldn't place her. They locked eyes for a moment, but Brianna stayed focused on her speech.

"Tell me, how many of you voted in the last election?" Brianna looked around the room, mentally noting that only about a third of those present raised their hands. Without wasting time, she resumed.

"The media says that hopelessness has stifled Rockville. They say that despair has it by the throat. People say the city is forgotten, especially the 5th District, that it's run down, too riddled with poverty and crime to be restored. I say that's untrue. I say that with a change in leadership and the teaching of the importance of politics as well as the role it plays in all of our lives, the city can be restored."

"That's right, that's right!" someone shouted.

Brianna made eye contact with one audience member after another as they applauded her. The response she was getting reminded her of that what she was accustomed to hearing in church. She scanned the room, her eyes meeting again with those of the woman all the way in the back.

"Don't let yourself be taken advantage of and manipulated. You've got to care enough about change to vote. Your vote does count. Your voice can be heard…" Brianna continued with her speech until she had everyone in the room riled up, awakening their emotions, and embedding in their ears her political views and daring them to vote—for her of course.

After she stepped off the stage, she made her way towards the back of the room, meeting with people individually, shaking hands, accepting compliments, and answering questions. With a closer look she knew exactly who the familiar-looking woman was. Her name was Pamela Thompson and she was the recently appointed treasurer of Rockville. She had taken over after her predecessor had been busted for illegal activity and ousted from his post. Pamela seized Brianna's attention.

"Hi." Pam had walked over to Brianna and introduced herself. "Pamela Thompson, city treasurer."

Brianna nodded and they shook hands. "Brianna Anderson, soon to be councilwoman." Their handshake was coupled with a soft gaze that lasted seconds longer than it should have. Their release lingered.

"So I heard." Pamela smiled. "Wonderful speech."

"Thank you." Brianna grinned while admiring how beautiful Pam was. She noticed that Sheldon was handing literature to people as they walked out. The room was nearly empty.

"Well, I have to get going. I just wanted to formally introduce myself." Pamela reached in her purse and handed Brianna a business card. "If you ever need anything, don't hesitate to give me a call."

Butterflies. Brianna felt a whir inside that she hadn't felt in a very long time. "Thanks." She didn't know what else to say. It could have been subtle flirting or it could have been networking. It could have been nothing. "It was a pleasure meeting you."

"Likewise." Pamela smiled and turned to walk out.

Brianna and Sheldon were among the last to leave the building. On the way to her next stop, she was only half listening to him. Her mind traveled back to Pamela. Brianna was intrigued by the woman who appeared to be older than she was but beautiful no less. Pam had been wearing a soft pink silk blouse under a light grey pant suit. Her smile was flawless.

"And don't let Smith get to you, Anderson." Sheldon was saying something about Colleen. "Just smile and be polite."

"I will." She snapped back into focus, redirecting her thoughts back to her campaign.

Chapter 4

"Okay, thanks for the heads up. I'll talk to you soon," Pamela said before hanging up. She dropped her cordless phone on the floor outside of her bathtub. After leaving the rally where she had heard Brianna speaking, she went back home. She wasn't sure why she went or why she flirted with Brianna. She wasn't sure of anything. Ever since Pamela had heard of Brianna, she'd been interested in her, and after seeing her up close and in person, Pam's attraction had been solidified. She'd been ignoring her feelings of desire for women for years, but every day it became harder and she didn't want to do it anymore.

A trail of Pam's clothes lay on the floor, and the medicine cabinet sat with its mirrored door slightly ajar. Alternating guitar and piano solos slow danced over a bluesy rhythm as she closed her eyes and relaxed, trying for the moment, to forget about work. Serenity began to embrace her as she lay in the large bathtub with a blanket of bubbles floating above her skin and salt crystals beneath her. Lavender-scented candles illuminated the room, and the temperature of the water was just hot enough to be soothing. *I wonder if she's involved...* Pam let her mind wander to Brianna. It had been nearly fourteen years since she had shared an intimate encounter with a woman. She'd been suppressing her desire for the sake of living a *normal* life and not giving her preaching father a heart attack. She sighed with a mix of sadness and enchantment, trying to clear her mind.

The pressure that she'd been feeling for months in her new position as city treasurer was finally gone. The revenue and cash flow reports were done. The new budget was complete, and everyone who worked under her was wholly aware of the way she wanted things to be done: honestly and accurately.

It had taken a lot of time and an unimaginable amount of energy for Pam to whip Rockville's treasury office into shape after her predecessor's scandal. Shortly after being appointed by the mayor and taking office, Pamela stared down the barrel of an immediate budget deficit of 140 million dollars, a cumulative budget deficit of almost 100 million dollars over five years, and a group of people who were still loyal to their former boss despite the fact that he'd left the city's accounts in shambles. Many disliked her because of her plan to reorganize the municipal workforce, which included cutting over 500 jobs and freezing wages for three years. Even though she wasn't popular among public sector workers, she was sure to hold her seat as treasurer because no one was running against her.

Brianna slid back into Pam's mind. She was absolutely beautiful and had an aggressive femininity that mesmerized Pam. After meeting her in person, she had a hopeful feeling that Brianna was a closet lesbian. It was in Brianna's eyes when they shared a gaze.

The sound of the garage door opening captured Pam's attention. Eric was home. She sighed and used her toes to pull the stopper out of the tub to release the water and stepped out. Minutes later he entered the house.

"Pam?" She heard his baritone voice as he came up the stairs. She should have met him at the door, but she didn't feel like it.

Slipping into her white terrycloth bathrobe, she took a deep breath before answering semi-enthusiastically. "Hi, honey!" She smiled when she saw him and walked into his arms. "I just got out of the tub."

Before he could respond, his cell phone rang. She hoped he would take the call but he didn't. He silenced it and hugged her tighter, and lifting her off her feet before kissing her deeply. "I missed you." Eric smelled good but needed a shave. His stubbly beard scratched her cheek as they embraced.

"Me too." She planted a soft, dry kiss on his cheek before slipping out of his hug.

He smiled. "Oh, I almost forgot. This is for you." He pulled a long, thin box out of his pants pocket.

Pamela's eyes widened in surprise when she opened it and saw a sparkling pink sapphire and diamond bracelet inside, "What's this for?"

"For putting up with my not being around much."

Still smiling about her gift, she nodded positively. "Okay."

"What's for dinner?"

Dinner? She hadn't cooked anything and was a little surprised that she hadn't remembered to. Her mind was too wrapped around Brianna to remember to go through the motions with Eric. She suggested that they go out to eat.

"Sure, we can do that." Eric continued and gave her a devilish smile. "What are the chances of your letting me have dessert before we go out?" He pulled her close to him again.

She recognized the yearning look in his hazel eyes and the sultry tone of his voice. She felt the solidness of his manhood against her as they held each other. Pamela was in the mood to be intimate but not with him. She couldn't say no though. He'd been gone for more than a week, and it would seem odd for her to deny him. She consented.

In Cherry Hill, Brianna was laying against Franklin's smooth, muscular chest as they watched a kung-fu film on his 50-inch plasma television. She'd gone to his place to tell him that she wanted to put an end to their sexual encounters but found it too difficult. When she arrived, he'd had dinner on the table and they ended up talking about work rather than their personal lives. A part of her wished she would have just done it over the phone, but she wanted to do it in person. She didn't want to cut him off completely; she just wanted to go back to being 'just friends.'

They'd both dozed off by the time the movie was over. The credits had finished rolling and the screen was black. The only sounds were the slight crackling of the gas fireplace and the quiet swish of water from his wall-mounted aquarium. A phone call startled them out of their sleep.

Frank reached for the telephone. "Hello?" He answered quietly. The muscles in his stomach tightened when he heard the voice on the other end.

Brianna woke up and got off him. She leaned back and stretched. As a yawn escaped her, she barely paid attention to him. She wanted to lie down in a bed.

"Yeah. Okay…sure." Franklin tried to keep his responses to Yesenia brief. He held the phone close to his ear to minimize the chance of Brianna hearing another woman's voice on the other end. "No problem. I'll catch up with you tomorrow. All right, bye."

Brianna became alert. She could tell from the way he spoke that it *was* another woman. She knew that much from his apparent guilt and silent uneasiness. She also assumed that he was sleeping with this woman. Frank's face was flush with panic. Brianna's initial reaction was anger, but she ingested it along with the thick, bitter taste of jealousy.

Trying to keep her composure, she inched away from him on the couch. "I um…I have a long day ahead of me, Frank." She stood up. "I'm going to head home." Brianna bit her bottom lip in self-restraint. Reality stung her. She knew she could be wrong, but her gut told her she was right.

"Wait, why don't you just stay the night, Bri?"

Because you're sleeping with someone else and it's taking all I have not to react to what I just found out! She exhaled. "No, I kind of want to be in my own bed."

Her response threw him off. He didn't know what to say. "Are you sure?"

"Yes." She walked toward the coat closet to retrieve her things.

Franklin followed her. He was antsy. The fact that she didn't question the phone call made him uncomfortable. Granted, he didn't want drama, but silence seemed to be worse. At least he would know what she was thinking if she questioned him.

Brianna turned to face him as she slipped into her jacket. "I'll call you, Frank." She gave him a thin smile and adjusted her clothes. "Okay?"

"All right." He leaned in to kiss her but she moved back, avoiding his lips.

"I'll call you," she said flatly and turned to leave.

Brianna got halfway to her car before tears started to fall. She was hurt. She was angry. She was jealous, and most of all, she was in denial. She kept walking to her car and tried to keep it together in case Franklin was watching her, which he probably was. She was aching. By the time she sat behind the wheel, she could no longer act as if she wasn't bothered. The tears flowed.

"How could he do this to me? How could he cheat?" She started her car. "*Him*? It's not his fault! We're not even a couple! Why did *I* do this to me?" Brianna cried and continued to ramble to herself as she drove home. She was upset with Franklin but angrier at herself. A funnel cloud of emotions whirled inside of her as she wondered how she could be hurt by a man with whom she didn't even want to continue sleeping. It was the betrayal. He had to have known that sleeping with another woman would hurt her regardless of whether or not they'd set boundaries, didn't he? They were friends. Wasn't that enough of a reason for him to consider her feelings? She was furious!

By the time she got into her condo, there were three messages from Frank on her cell phone voice mail and two on her home service asking her to call him. He felt guilty and she knew it. She knew that she was guilty as well. If she cut things off with him now, there was no way to tell how things would unfold over the remaining weeks until Election Day. Though difficult, she decided to subordinate her feelings for the time being and remain focused on her career.

Chapter 5

Brianna ignored the revelation that there was another woman and didn't bring it up to Frank the next evening. She used all of her strength to keep her personal problems separate from her campaign and stay focused on work.

"Thank you." The attendees gave her a round of applause after she completed her speech at a community center.

She stepped away from the podium and posed for a photograph with Franklin and Terrence. They held an endorsement they helped her get from a local coalition of professionals and entrepreneurs who wanted to see Rockville thrive again.

After taking the photo, Brianna shook everyone's hand and then the three of them made a swift exit from the main room and into an alcove. Her chemistry with Frank was off, but she didn't say anything, neither did he. He reeked of anxiety, however.

"Just excuse me for a moment. I need to go to the ladies room." Brianna was angry with Frank. She had worked hard all night to conceal it and was struggling to continue. She turned from them quickly and walked away before her feelings pushed themselves to the surface.

Sheldon walked into the alcove and greeted the guys. "Thanks, fellas. We really appreciate all of the support you've given."

"It's no problem at all. We believe in her," Franklin responded.

Sheldon's cell phone rang. "Excuse me," he said stepping away to take the call in private.

"What's up with you tonight?" Terrence questioned Frank as soon as they were alone.

"Nothing, why?"

"Something is up. You're not yourself."

"Nah, I'm fine, man." Franklin tapped his hand against his leg.

"Did something happen between you and Brianna?" He quizzed. "Now that I think about it, something is the matter with both of you."

"T, I'm cool."

Brianna emerged, walking toward them while checking her PDA.

"Let it go, man." Frank spoke quietly as she approached.

Terrence wasn't satisfied. "Yeah, I'll let it go for now."

Sheldon walked back over to them. "Something came up at home that I have to tend to."

"Okay." Brianna was caught off guard by his abruptness.

"You did an excellent job tonight as usual, Anderson. I'll see you in the morning," Sheldon added.

"See you," she responded.

Sheldon left and shortly after, Brianna, Frank and Terrence exited the building.

"Terrence, thanks again for all of your help. I appreciate it more than you know." Brianna smiled at him.

"You're welcome." He paused before speaking again. "Well, I have to get going too. Frank, I'll catch up with you tomorrow."

"All right, later, man."

"Thank you too, Franklin." Brianna only looked at him for a second before gazing away.

"Bri, you know I'd do anything for you."

There was an awkward silence. He wanted to talk about the previous night but was afraid to. He knew that she knew that something was going on, but he wasn't sure of what would happen if the truth were spoken aloud.

"I'm pretty tired." Brianna broke the quiet.

"Want to call it a night?"

"Yeah, I think that's best." She stepped closer to him and put her arms loosely around him. "I'll call you."

"Okay."

The two went their separate ways. Brianna tried her best to put him out of her mind. She took deep breaths and held back tears as she drove home.

"Keep it together," she told herself.

Where is your self-respect—your personal morals? Her inner voice tormented her as she thought about her decision to remain silent about Frank's pseudo-infidelity. It was not uncommon for Brianna to sacrifice her feelings for her career. It was becoming an ugly pattern in her life that only she could see. It stared her in the face every morning when she looked in the mirror and was an embarrassing reflection of reality.

As she pulled into her parking space her mind wandered to Pamela, the city treasurer who had introduced herself to Brianna over a week ago. She thought about calling her but was unsure. What would she say?

A few moments went by with Brianna sitting in her parked car. Slumped forward with her arms draped across the steering wheel, she stared up at a beautiful, starlit sky before deciding to go up to her condo.

With every step, Brianna felt a bit more compelled to call Pamela. She wasn't sure if it was courage, stupidity, loneliness, or pent-up frustration that was making her want to do it, but soon after she got in the door, she found herself rifling through her purse to locate Pam's card. She found it and stared at it. It had a cell phone number on it.

"I need a drink first," she mumbled to herself as she walked into the kitchen.

As she poured herself a glass of red wine, she tried to come up with a good reason for calling. *I'll just ask her to lunch…to talk politics.* It seemed easiest to throw her an invitation about work. She picked up the phone and dialed quickly before she lost her nerve. She paced while waiting for an answer. She took another sip of wine and continued to pace.

"Pamela Thompson." Her feminine voice filled the line.

Brianna couldn't speak immediately. Nervous silence halted a response.

"Hello?" Pamela spoke again.

"Hi," Brianna cleared her throat. "Pamela."

"Yes, this is she. May I ask whose calling?"

"This is Brianna…Ander—"

"Anderson, city council hopeful." Pam helped Brianna find her words.

"Yes, it's me."

They shared a laugh at the awkward beginning of the call.

"Call me Pam."

"Okay, Pam then. I was just wondering what your schedule looked like this week…" She wanted to hurry up and put the invitation on the table. "…if you have a free afternoon for lunch?"

In her living room, Pam leaned back on the love seat and smiled. She had been hoping to hear from the budding politician since giving Brianna her contact information. "I'm not looking at my schedule at the moment, but I'm sure I can make time. Is there anything in particular that you want to talk about over lunch?"

"Oh…just work, politics… maybe your experience if you don't mind sharing."

"I don't."

"Great, so should I call you tomorrow to set the date?" Brianna beamed! She felt like a teenager.

"Yes, you can call me in the morning."

"All right. I'll do that."

They both knew their conversation should close, but there was a dwelling silence on the line as neither of them wanted to initiate the end of the call.

"Do you have to hang up now?" Pam picked it back up this time.

"No, I don't."

"Well, we can talk now if you want."

"Okay." Brianna sat down, sipped her wine and smiled.

"So…your campaign seems to be going great. I do wish you the best in your bid."

"Thank you."

"Council could use a woman like you."

"Really," Brianna said, thinking about Pam's statement. "What's a woman like me?"

"Confident, intelligent, poised, focused and strong." Pam spoke matter-of-factly. *And beautiful.*

"Thanks." Brianna had not been prepared for the rush of compliments but accepted them with ease. "You've certainly done a great job as the new treasurer. I can only imagine the pressure you faced taking over after someone who was eclipsed by a scandal."

"Thank you. It's not an easy job," Pam said. "So what would you like to know about me?"

"Anything you're willing to share…"

"Hmm. That's pretty broad, but I can start with the basics. Of course you know I'm the city treasurer and though extremely difficult, I do love my job. I'm married with no children…"

Brianna chuckled. "I'm sorry. I don't mean to interview you."

"It's all right. What about you, Anderson?" She paused. "Brianna, sorry I'm not accustomed to calling you by your first name."

"It's okay. To answer your question though, my career has a hundred percent of my focus right now. A seat on council is something I want very badly."

"I'm sorry, Brianna. Can you hold on for a second?"

"Sure." Brianna could hear the muted sounds of Pam and a man, her husband, she assumed.

The two women didn't get a chance to converse much longer as Pam brought their phone call to an end when she returned to the line.

"Hi, my husband is home. I should go now. It was a pleasure speaking with you, Anderson."

"Likewise, so I'll call you in the morning to schedule lunch." Her statement sounded more like a question.

"You've got it."

"All right. Have a good evening."

"You too."

Brianna hung up the phone feeling enchanted by the possibilities of what could happen with Pam. She knew that her thoughts were jumping far ahead of where they should be after an initial conversation, but she had a gut feeling that told her that Pam was closeted, and like Brianna, was deeply yearning to be with a woman. The thought of being emotionally involved and intimate with a woman again produced vibrations within Brianna that she hadn't experienced in almost a decade. She closed her eyes and exhaled.

"Relax," she told herself and got up to put away the glass and bottle of wine. "Just relax."

Her mind was racing despite her wishes. Besides Pam, Franklin was on her mind. She was still hurt by his actions and wanted to end things with him. "Just tell him you want to be friends," she said to herself.

As the words fell from her lips the telephone rang. The caller ID showed it was Franklin. She stared at the phone as it rang, debating if she wanted to deal with him at that moment. She bit her bottom lip and thought about it. *Do it and get it over with*!

Brianna decided to send the call to voice mail, promising herself that she would tell him the following day. She didn't want to go to bed on a depressed note after being stirred up by her conversation with Pam. She was looking forward to calling Pam in the morning and setting up their lunch date, and she'd much rather have Pam be the last thing on her mind than Frank. She replaced the cordless phone on the hook, turned off the lights, and retired for the night.

Chapter 6

The next morning started off horribly.

"This is a disgrace!" Brianna threw the daily newspaper into a nearby garbage can. Her eyes were intense as she anxiously paced her headquarters.

"Don't worry, Anderson." Sheldon sat perched on the edge of his seat. "The race is still close and you have a very good shot at winning."

Brianna exhaled and rubbed her forehead. Her opponent had just unleashed a new wave of below-the-belt ads.

"I didn't come this far to lose." She glanced in the trash at the cartoon of her being depicted as an unnoticed, curious child who wasn't tall enough to sit at a big table with her opponent and others members of city council. "I've got to work smarter," she said before glancing outside a corner window. She could see an American flag waving in the ashen sky over Rockville—the home of dirty politics.

Sheldon walked toward her. "All you need is one more vote than she gets. Besides, I have more brainpower in one testicle than Smith and her campaign manager together. Don't worry, we're going to make it so the majority of the voters in the district trust you."

"How, Shel? There's a chance that I won't—"

"Are you questioning your candidacy?" He cut her off. "This can't be the Anderson I've been working with. No, hell no!"

"No, it's just….I don't know." She walked back over to her desk and sat down.

Sheldon followed her. "Is everything okay, Anderson? I mean, besides the obvious."

"Everything is fine." She sighed.

"You sure?"

"Yes." Dressed in a light blue skirt suit and white blouse, she leaned back in her chair and stared at the wall calendar. She wore small teardrop-shaped pearl earrings and a matching single string around her neck. "We have to leave soon, don't we?"

"Yes. Time spent in here is a big waste for you. You need to be out meeting as many people as possible."

One of her volunteers walked in. "Excuse me, Brianna?"

"Yes, Asad?"

He handed her loose pages. "I finished making the corrections to your speech for you."

"Thank you."

"You're welcome," he said and turned and walked out.

Brianna looked at her watch and spoke to Sheldon. "I just need a few minutes to gather myself and then I'll be ready to go."

"Brianna?" Yesenia interrupted her this time.

"Yes?"

"I'm not feeling well. I think I'm going to call it a day if it's all right with you."

"That's fine, Yesenia. Take care of yourself."

"I will, thanks."

Yesenia walked out and Sheldon's eyes followed her. He was distracted by her.

"Shel?" Brianna demanded his attention.

"Yes, sorry."

"Just give me a few minutes, okay?"

"All right. Oh, by the way, I have someone who is going to film your speech tonight so we can upload it to YouTube."

"That's great, thanks. Hopefully that can reach some of the younger residents and get them to pay attention to the election. Can you think of something else to reach older people?"

"I'm already working on it. I told you not to fret. I'll be back in a little bit." Sheldon winked and walked out.

Her mood seemed to lighten when she was alone. She began thinking of Pam and decided to call her. The phone rang continuously before going to voice mail. Brianna left her a brief message gently reminding Pam about setting a lunch date and an open invitation for a callback before hanging up.

She placed the phone down and looked over the pages that Asad had given her.

"Hey." Sheldon re-entered smelling of cigarettes.

"Hey."

"Are you ready to head out?"

"Yeah, let's go," she said and grabbed her belongings. She had a full day of appearances and was scheduled to deliver a speech to the local chapter of the League of Women Voters.

It was a hazy day in Rockville. Driving down random streets one could see a never-ending maze of abandoned buildings, many of which had burnt-out frames and graffiti scrawled across them—windows busted out, replaced by wood or nothing at all. The picture of poverty was painted on the faces of the residents as they walked along trash-littered streets, some of which were lined by old kitchen appliances. Vacant spaces in between homes housed knee-high grass, random pieces of dirty old furniture, and stray dogs. The district was a mix of brick row houses, wooden shacks, and every now and then, decent houses not surrounded by rubbish but having iron bars around the porches and windows for the safety of the owners.

Brianna peered out of the window silently as Sheldon drove. She focused on her tasks for the day and tried to think of strategies to stay ahead in the race.

Later that day Franklin met with Yesenia at his home. Dressed in a crisp, white dress shirt and navy slacks, he sat on the corner of the desk in his home office. His tie was loosened about his neck.

"I can't do this anymore, Yesenia. I'm sorry."

"Why? What do you mean you can't do this anymore? What's wrong?" She was clearly unhappy with his statement.

"I just can't. It doesn't feel right. It's not you, it's me."

"Oh, give me a break! It's Brianna!"

"Well, yes and no. Anyway, I don't want to fight about this." He stood up.

Losing Control

"I'm not fighting! I'm just saying…" she walked over to him. "I don't want to stop seeing you, Frank. Why is it such a big deal? She doesn't even know! We've been doing this all month and all of a sudden it's not right?" Yesenia stormed away from him and walked toward the door, but he didn't follow her. "Just like that huh, Frank? You just use me and leave me?"

"I did not use you! You came on to *me!*"

"Well, if you're so concerned with Brianna's feelings, why are you sleeping with me?" She walked back over to him.

"I don't know. It was a mistake."

"Mistake my ass. What kind of mistake happens over and over, huh Papi? That's bullshit!"

He knew it was bullshit but wanted to rid himself of the guilt. There were many reasons for ending it, but he didn't think she needed to know all of them.

"Come on, Frank." She touched his face and kissed him. "I don't want to tie you down or anything. I just want to continue experiencing you." She got closer to him, kissed him again, and groped him. "Please."

He cleared his throat. "Yesenia…"

"Shhh." She kissed him and unzipped his slacks. "Don't talk."

Franklin felt her soft, warm hand reaching into his boxers and beginning to stroke him into an erection. He took a step back. "No, come on, Yesenia. Don't make this harder than it has to be."

"Tell me you don't like how it feels and I'll stop."

"I…"

"You can't admit it so why mess up a good thing, baby?"

He closed his eyes, turning to steel in her hands against his will. "No!" Frank regained control of himself and pulled her up. "I can't. We shouldn't. I'm sorry. Stop it."

"You know what? Fuck it. This so stupid! I don't even know why I'm begging you. It's your loss, Frank. It's your loss!" She shoved him.

He stood stiffly, staring at her with unwavering eyes that were strong enough to eliminate the need for him to dignify her violent gesture.

She rolled her eyes and started to leave.

"Yesenia," he called.

"What?"

Quickly humbled, he swallowed hard before speaking. "You're not going to say anything to Brianna are you?" He was worried.

She sucked her teeth.

"Well?"

"No, Frank. As much as I would like tell all, I'm not going to because I don't want *my* business out there like that. I'm thinking about my career too." Her honesty was soiled by the contempt in her voice.

Frank nodded. "Okay."

"Yeah, whatever, Frank." Yesenia sighed and left.

He was fatigued and annoyed and had a rock hard erection adding to the problem. A part of him wished he let her please him *before* telling her to leave, but he was tired of going through the motions and knew that it would only make things more complicated by sleeping with her again.

He decided to take matters into his own hands for the sake of relieving himself. Frank pulled out a magazine from a stack that he kept neatly tucked away at the bottom of a file cabinet of his home office and went into the bedroom to finish what Yesenia had started.

Hours later, Frank was awakened by a ringing telephone. Half dressed, he stumbled out of bed and clumsily looked around his room for his cordless phone.

"Hello?" He glanced at the digital clock on the nightstand. He had slept past 7:00.

"Hey, Frank." It was Terrence.

"What's up, man?"

"Not much. I'm bored."

Franklin chuckled. "What do you expect me to do about it?"

"I don't know. I mean, I have work to do, but I just don't feel like it. Do you want to go to a bar, have a couple of beers, and shoot pool or something?"

"Yeah, why not? There's nothing going on over here anyway." Franklin walked over to his closet to look for something to wear. Now awake, he was relaxed despite the earlier drama with Yesenia.

"All right," Terrence said. "Let's meet up at Golden Cue."

"Cool. How about catching up in a half an hour or so?" Frank pulled a pair of jeans out of his closet.

"Sounds like a plan."

"Okay, see you then."

"Later," said Terrence.

Frank hung up the phone and changed clothes. A night out of the house would do him some good, he decided. He knew that if he stayed in, he'd either work until late in the night or sit up thinking about his relationship problems. He didn't want to do either.

In Rockville, Brianna was wrapping up a speech to an interactive audience of women. She felt energized and confident as she gave her closing remarks.

"What's happening in Rockville is critical for us. It's bad for our health. It's disastrous for our children and the next generation. We are becoming lost and forgotten, stuck in bleak insomnia, never experiencing the American Dream. We have to take a stand!"

Applause.

Brianna felt good about her campaign again. She managed to have an excellent day at all of her scheduled appearances. As she spoke with people after giving her speech, thoughts of Pam scampered through her mind. She had to keep cautioning herself not to dream up any possibilities of what *could* be because there was a strong possibility that nothing would ever be. She didn't even have confirmation that Pam was interested in her romantically. And then there was the fact that Pam was married.

"You've got my vote, Anderson!" An audience member brought Brianna back to reality.

"Thank you so much," she replied and smiled.

She greeted a few more people before making an exit with Sheldon. After returning to headquarters, they went their separate ways. As she drove to her condo, she checked her missed calls and voice mail. She was delighted to hear that one of the messages was from Pam. The others were from Frank and her mother.

Frank had called to let her know that he was able to raise some more funds for her campaign and that he had some people he wanted her to meet. His voice saddened her. She didn't even want to think about her situation with him at the moment and decided to call Pam back.

"Brianna, hello," Pam answered. She was smiling.
"I got your message. Tomorrow afternoon is fine with me."
"Great. So I'll see you at one o'clock?"
"Yes, you will." Brianna grinned.
"All right, then it's set. I do have to go now. I have a bit of work I'm trying to get done tonight."
"No problem. I've had a busy day myself. I'll see you tomorrow and will call if anything comes up."
"Sounds good." Pam responded.
"Bye."
"Goodnight."

Brianna hung up the phone and then returned her mother's call. She was always comforted when she spoke with her. Mrs. Anderson always had a way of reassuring her daughter that she was doing the right thing and was on the right path. She was always so proud of Brianna and who she had become. Brianna missed how close they used to be when she lived in New York.

She arrived at home and was undressing in her condo as she continued talking to her mother. The two of them and her grandmother were very close when Brianna was younger. They all lived in the same housing project. When Brianna was old enough to need her own space, her mother moved in with her grandmother and gave Brianna the vacated apartment. The two older women always encouraged Brianna to study hard and be the one to make it out of the projects. They knew of her sexuality and it didn't bother them. It did, however, bother them that she didn't have the courage to be herself when she left home, but they understood her decision.

"I love you too, Mom," said Brianna. "Tell Grandma I love her and I'll call again soon."

She said goodnight and hung up amazed that she was only a two-hour drive away but felt much farther. After settling in comfortably for the evening, she finally called Franklin back.

"Brianna, hey!" Frank sounded happy when he answered the phone.

"Hi Frank, I got your message. That's great news about the fundraising. Thank you so much!"

"You're welcome. How was your day?"

"It was pretty good—a lot of meetings, you know, the usual. How about yours?"

"It was rough. I'm just glad it's over." There was a brief pause in their conversation before Franklin picked it back up. "Hey, do you think we can meet up tomorrow?"

"Um, sure."

"Can I come over there or do you want to go out?"

"You can come over here." As they continued to chat, Brianna thought about telling him how she was feeling. She wanted to say she was hurt by his actions, but she didn't.

"What time?"

Brianna was lost in her thoughts.

"Hello?" Frank spoke again.

"I'm sorry, I spaced out. What did you say?"

He laughed. "I said what time should I come over?"

"I'm not sure yet. I'll call you during the day and let you know."

"All right."

"You know Frank..." Brianna began and paused.

"Yeah?"

"I've been thinking." Before she could ponder her feelings anymore, she began speaking them as if forced to do so. "I um..."

"What?"

"I was thinking that maybe you and I should slow down—romantically, you know? I just...I have a lot on my plate right now and I want to stay focused on the race and..." she went on, astonished at how easily she was breaking things off with him right after he said he had raised more money for her, but she hoped he would have done that even if they had never slept together. Wouldn't a real friend who had the means to help do so without sexual enticement?

Frank listened to her. He wasn't completely surprised and wasn't sure what to say. He knew that something had to give with Brianna after the phone call incident. He just didn't know how it would manifest. As he listened to her excuses for stopping the sexual encounters, he became upset but agreed to go back to being just friends. That's the way they started and it was most important to him.

"If that's what you want, Brianna. Of course." He spoke softly. He was ready to end the day, which seemed to be bottomless and only going from bad to worse.

"Okay." Brianna didn't know what else to say.

"I want you to be happy."

"Thank you," she said.

"And I want you to know that I'll still do everything I can to help you win the election."

She was relieved. "Thank you, Franklin! I know everything feels awkward now. I just...I guess I just. I don't know, you know? I've felt that way for a while, but didn't know how it would impact our friendship."

"I see," he said.

"Well, it's getting late."

"Yeah, it is. Do you still want me to come over tomorrow or no? I could just set up a meeting with the people I wanted to connect you with," he said. He wanted to get off the phone.

"Okay, let's do that. I'm sorry the night ended like this."

"Don't worry about it, Bri. It's cool."

She could tell he was upset but wasn't going to take back what she had said. It was long overdue. "I'll call you tomorrow then."

"All right."

"Night, Frank."

"Night, Brianna."

Brianna hung up the phone and went out to her balcony that overlooked the Delaware River and Philadelphia skyline. Her condo was relatively new and was built as a part the city's revitalization effort to capitalize on Rockville's waterfront. Just five years earlier, a prison filled with 1,000 inmates stood at her current location. If they didn't see eye-to-eye on anything else, all of the local politicians agreed the prison needed to be demolished, and the inmates moved.

She sat down and stared up at the stars, trying to relax the flurry inside of her. She hoped the cool night air would clear her mind and help her develop a plan for finding a healthy balance between work, life, and love. Without Frank around, the nights would become lonelier but more honest. She would be forced to deal with her suppressed desires.

Chapter 7

The next morning Brianna was in the ladies room at her headquarters when she heard sniffling coming from one of the stalls. She ignored it at first, but when it became clear that someone was crying, she spoke up.

"Are you okay?" Brianna said aloud but got no answer. She thought about asking again but decided against it. She shrugged and began washing her hands.

The stall door opened and Yesenia walked out teary-eyed and disheveled.

"Hey, Yesenia, what's the matter?" Brianna was surprised. She had never seen her in such a state before.

"Nothing," she lied. "I'm fine."

"You can tell me. What's wrong?"

Yesenia sighed. "It's…relationship problems."

"Oh." Brianna didn't know if she should probe or not.

Yesenia stared at her but didn't say anything else.

"Do you want to talk about it?"

"I'll be fine," she said and paused.

Brianna stepped closer to her and put her hand on Yesenia's shoulder. "Sometimes talking about it helps."

Brianna was the last person she wanted to talk to, but pain was brewing inside her. "It just hurts, you know?" Yesenia took a deep breath before speaking again. She debated talking about Frank.

"What is it?" Brianna asked.

"I just broke up with someone. We weren't serious or anything, but I was hoping that we could get to that point," she paused. "He didn't want to though. Another woman has his attention." Yesenia let the words flow.

"Oh, I'm sorry. I know that must hurt."

"More than you know."

"Well," said Brianna. "I know that nothing but time really heals broken hearts, but if there is anything I can do to make your days here better, let me know."

Yesenia looked Brianna directly in her brown eyes but remained silent.

"It'll be okay," Brianna continued. "Things always find a way to work themselves out somehow."

"Yeah." Yesenia reached for a paper towel to dry her eyes. "I'll be fine. Thanks for listening," Yesenia was angry. She wanted to scream at Brianna for being in the way of her getting Frank.

"Anytime." Brianna's cell phone rang, pulling her out of the moment. "I have to take this," she said.

"All right." Yesenia gave Brianna a lifeless smile.

Brianna took the call and walked out of the ladies room. Yesenia didn't know how long she could keep up the charade, but she knew that Brianna wouldn't let Frank go so easily. She looked in the mirror and took a few moments to get herself together before leaving the bathroom. It would take planning, but she was determined to get Franklin all to herself without jeopardizing her position on the campaign or risking all the connections she was making while working for Brianna. She too had her career on her mind, though her love life was reaching its tentacles into it. Whatever her next move, it had to be calculated before being executed.

Inside the main room of the headquarters, Sheldon entered wearing a leather messenger bag slung over his shoulder and carrying a cup of coffee in one hand.

"Hey, you." Brianna said. "You're late. You're supposed to be driving me to the debate."

"I know. I know. I'm sorry. Are you ready?"

Losing Control

"Yes," she said, and glanced at her watch. "I want to get it over with."

Brianna was scheduled for a mid-morning debate, with her opponent, at a local college. It was to be aired live on local cable television.

"All right, let's head out." Sheldon turned around just as quickly as he had walked in, sipping his coffee.

They got in his shiny black SUV and left to go to the campus.

"This is only scheduled for an hour, right?" Brianna asked. She had a lunch date with Pam and didn't want to be late.

"Yes, give or take an extra half an hour for Q&A."

"Okay."

As Brianna and Sheldon drove to their destination, they went over key points for her to remember during the debate. She was confident about the planned topics but wanted to be sure she didn't stumble over random questions that an audience member might throw out or even a challenging comment from Smith.

"Just remember," Sheldon spoke, "if someone gets off topic, find a way to answer in a way that will bring the dialog back to your campaign platform, revitalizing District 5. The best thing you can do is remain consistent. People want someone who doesn't flip-flop. They want someone who doesn't waver."

"Mm hm. I'll be fine." Brianna was ready. She felt competitive.

At Rockville City Hall, Pamela closed her office door to take a call from her husband. "I'm so swamped here today, Eric."

He wanted to meet for lunch. "What time do you think you'll wrap up? How about going out to dinner instead?"

"I don't know, but I'll try to get out of here as soon as possible."

"Okay. Just give me a call later and let me know."

Someone knocked at Pam's door.

"I will. Eric, baby, I have to go now. I'll call you back."

"All right. Talk to you later."

"Goodbye."

Pam hung up and called for the person at her door to come in. A stout man with walnut skin and a thick mustache walked in carrying two manila folders.

"I have a few things for you to look over." His voice was heavy, filled with bass.

"Thanks." She took the documents from him. "What are they?"

"Reports on last month's welfare SSI distribution and a suggested reconciliation. The numbers are off."

"All right, I'll review them."

He looked at her and smiled.

"Is that all?" Pam asked.

"Yes. That's all." He turned to walk out.

She couldn't stand him. He had a reputation for being sleazy and making unwanted passes at the women, but no one had formed an official complaint against him. She rolled her eyes at the thought of him and pulled a page out of the welfare folder and stared at the numbers.

Pam skimmed the figures and put them aside to review later that afternoon. She glanced at the clock in her small, mahogany-paneled office and turned her attention back to the 100 e-mails in her inbox. She wanted to get through them before lunchtime. She was looking forward to seeing Brianna.

In a crowded college auditorium, Brianna stole a look at the time as she went back and forth with Smith.

"...and I think each and every person needs to be intellectually independent enough to think and act for him—or herself based on the facts. All I did was state the truth about the current state of the 5th District, to which Ms. Smith belongs, and share my proposals for changes should *I* be elected. I am not here to spew personal attacks on unrelated matters as my opponent has done. Ms. Smith claims that her experience is an asset, but if that's the case, why is Rockville in its current condition?"

She looked at Smith and continued speaking. "This would be my first time holding a seat, but unlike Ms. Smith, my emotions are removed from this debate. Just the facts are on the table as far as I'm concerned." Brianna paused and looked at the moderator. "I hope that answers your question."

Brianna was paradoxically nervous and confident. She had fumbled a question about zoning but hoped the way she handled the final ones would overpower her lackluster response to the earlier question.

A few more inquiries were taken before the debate was brought to a close. Journalists took pictures of Colleen and Brianna as they left the auditorium. When she arrived back at her headquarters, Brianna debriefed with Sheldon and then slipped out for her lunch with Pam.

"I'll be back," she called as she grabbed her purse and walked toward the door.

"Mm hmm. There's work to be done, Anderson."

"I know," she said as she walked out, passing Yesenia on her way. They acknowledged each other but that was all.

Brianna got in her car and drove to a Mexican restaurant on the other side of the Ben Franklin Bridge in Philadelphia. She and Pam arrived within seconds of each other and greeted with a handshake and a smile.

"Hi." Brianna spoke first. "It's nice to see you again."

Pam held the door open for her. "Likewise. How are you?" She was dressed in a black skirt suit with a red blouse. Her hair evenly fell by her shoulders with one side tucked behind her ear. Her make-up made her dark complexion look naturally flawless, and her eyes were spellbinding in their simple beauty.

"I'm well, and you?"

"I'm good…glad to take a break from work."

"Tell me about it," Brianna added. "I hardly ever take one. I don't think I've actually taken a real lunch *break* in weeks."

Pam was captivated by Brianna's smooth, light brown skin and adorable dimples. Brianna had her hair pulled back and styled elegantly. She wore a charcoal pantsuit with a silver silk blouse accented by dainty white gold jewelry.

"Party of two?" the greeter asked.

"Yes," Pam answered. She glanced at Brianna, who nodded and agreed.

"Follow me." The greeter led them to a corner table.

Moments after they were seated, their waiter came over. "Good afternoon, ladies," he said and placed two glasses on the table. "Would you like mineral, sparkling, or tap water?"

"Mineral is fine," Brianna answered.

Pam concurred.

"All right, I'll be right back." He smiled and walked away.

"Fast service," Pam said, keeping their conversation going.

"Yep, that's one of the best things about this place."

Pam and Brianna shared a few minutes of small talk and then shifted their conversation to work. By the time the waiter arrived with their lunch, however, they were chatting about their personal lives. Brianna learned that Pam had been married to Eric for 12 years and had no children. He was an actuary and senior consultant for a human resources services firm in Philadelphia.

"Eric travels a lot," Pam said. "Most of the time, when I'm not working, I'm alone."

"Is it all work-related?"

"Yeah, mostly. He goes out looking for new business."

"I see."

"What about you?" Pam inquired.

"No husband, no kids. It's just my career and me."

Pam was silent.

"For now, at least," Brianna picked back up. "I guess. I don't know." She couldn't get her words to flow smoothly and could hear her heart beating when their conversation paused.

Pam looked Brianna in the eyes, searching. She wanted to skip the uncomfortable beginning but didn't know how. She could have been wrong about Brianna's sexuality but doubted it. Nevertheless, she had to be careful in getting the truth about her to come out.

"How is everything?" The waiter returned. He had perfect timing to patch the moment of awkward silence.

"Great, thank you," they both responded.

"Very good."

He smiled and walked away. Brianna glanced at her watch as they finished eating.

"Time goes by too fast when you're relaxing," Pam said.

"I thought it was when you were having fun," Brianna quipped.

Pam grinned. "Of course, that too. Are you?"

"What?"

"Having fun?"

"Yes, actually I am. It's amazing what a break can do."

"Oh, I know. I'm sure to have my rejuvenation days. Either at home or an hour at the spa; I *have* to have them or I'd go crazy from the stress. You should treat yourself sometime."

Brianna thought about it. "Hmm. Can you recommend a place?"

"As a matter of fact, I can. There's one in Moorestown that I've been a regular at for about a year now. It's called Heaven."

"Thanks. I'll look into it. Maybe I'll see you there one day."

"Or we could go together." *Shit. That was too forward,* Pam thought. She cursed herself for the gaffe.

Brianna smiled, following Pam's lead. "We could. Maybe I won't procrastinate going if we made an appointment together."

"Then why don't we do that?" Pam asked, feeling warm from Brianna's suggestion. She relaxed. "I think I'm already scheduled for an hour massage next Sunday."

"That sounds great. I'll check my schedule and let you know."

"Sounds good."

Their waiter returned to clear the table. "Did you want to see the dessert menu?"

Brianna and Pam looked at each other before declining.

"Just the check please," Brianna said. She didn't want to end lunch but knew she had to get going.

"I guess we better get back to work."

"Yes, we should. I enjoyed the conversation though. I managed not to check my e-mail the entire time!"

"Oh, you're one of those addicts."

Brianna blushed.

"It's okay. Most people are. I try not to become a slave to it."

"I try too, but it's hard. I can't help myself."

"Well, if I were in your shoes, I would probably be the same. You're in the middle of a campaign, Anderson. That's different."

"Brianna," she reminded Pam.

"Of course, I'm sorry." Now it was Pam's turn to blush.

The waiter returned with the check, which Pam insisted on picking up. They talked a little while longer while waiting for the receipt and then left. Back on the road, Brianna grinned, replaying the conversation in her mind. Meanwhile, Pam smiled as she drove back to her office at City Hall. She couldn't remember the last time she had felt so excited and anxious. She wanted to see Brianna again and soon.

As Brianna maneuvered her way back to her headquarters, she became lost in her thoughts of Pam. She thought about the spa invitation and couldn't wait to take her up on it. It was laced with a hint of seduction that swept Brianna into an existence in which she hadn't been in years. She welcomed it. She felt adventurous. Unconsciously escaping into the intoxicating possibilities of what could happen with Pam, Brianna became further enthralled. Things seemed to be happening slow, yet fast. She tried to tell herself that it was nothing and it was all innocent conversation, but she knew better.

Both women felt an underlying sexual tension shifting like an undercurrent. Their suppression of sexual and romantic desires was building, ready to rise and crash against the surface.

"Anderson! Nice of you to join us." Sheldon's booming voice was the first thing Brianna heard when she got back to her headquarters.

"Oh, Sheldon give me a break," she said and gave him a playful push.

"It's my job to give you shit and keep you on your toes."

"Yeah, don't I know it? Anyway, what did I miss? My pre-election financial reporting was done on time, right?" she asked after looking at the calendar on the wall.

"Yes, I took care of it."

"Thank you."

"Mm hm. Don't worry. I run an organized campaign. Stuff like that won't ever get by me even if *you* don't remember until after the due date." He teased.

She smiled. "That's why you're my manager."

"By the way, there are a couple of coffee shops and other places that you need to stop by over the next few days. Yesenia or one of the other volunteers is working on the schedule, and it'll be good face-to-face time with voters."

"Okay, just tell me when and where and I'll be there."

"Asad will shuttle you so you don't waste time driving around looking for parking spots."

"Great!"

"And the gays are having a dinner you might want to attend. Actually, you need to go. You can't afford to ignore them."

"The gays?" Brianna chuckled.

"Garden State Equality. They're having a dinner to get more involvement in their organization from South Jersey," he said. "Thinking of your career long-term, you should start being an ally with them now. You can't ignore their power and growing influence on the state."

She nodded, feeling embarrassed to hear Sheldon tell *her,* a closeted lesbian, that she shouldn't ignore gay people. She was ashamed of herself for being too much of a coward to come out and truly help the gay and lesbian community. Although New Jersey was a progressive state, the southern region was not as liberal as the north, and just like race and religion, sexuality mattered even though people acted as though it didn't.

"I'll look into that tomorrow and see if it's not too late to get you on the list or get you a ticket or whatever you need to attend."

"All right, Shel. Thanks."

"Okay. Hey, I need to run some personal errands so I'll see you later. Call me if you need anything or if something urgent comes up."

"I will."

Sheldon left and Brianna felt conflict wrestling inside of her.

As she continued to work through the next couple of days, it became apparent that *getting* new voters registered and to the polls on Election Day was going to be just as much of a challenge as trying to grab Smith's supporters and the undecided. The grim reality was that only 27 percent of 5th District residents voted. The key, she knew, was to reach the unreachable, touch the untouchable—be the candidate who made residents feel their votes meant something.

Thoughts of Pam swam through her mind alongside politics, stroking her imagination with tantalizing thoughts of exhilarating passion. The more submerged Brianna became in her work, the more a thought of Pam would became a breath of fresh air. They had spoken again after their lunch date and had scheduled a girls' day at the spa. Brianna was eagerly anticipating the experience.

Chapter 8

"That's game," Terrence said after knocking the eight ball into a corner pocket. He and Frank had just finished two games of pool. Terrence had won both.

"You're lucky I'm having an off night." Frank drank his last sip of beer and tossed the dark brown bottle into a nearby trashcan.

"It's not luck, its skill, boy. Now who's your daddy," Terrence joked.

Frank laughed and replaced his pool stick on the rack against the wall. "That's enough for me."

"Fine. You've taken enough of a beating for one night. Want another round on me?" Terrence nodded toward the bar.

"No, I'm good. Thanks, man."

"Suit yourself," he said and then turned to walk over to the bar. He signaled the bartender and ordered another drink. "Another rum and Coke, thanks." He sat down as soon as a seat became free.

Frank followed him. "Actually, yeah, get me another beer." He stood next to Terrence at the crowded bar. The atmosphere was dim and the sound of clinking glasses stood above the loud chatter of patrons.

Terrence looked up at Frank curiously. "Hey, you know you never told me what happened with you and Brianna."

"There wasn't much to tell. Nothing happened. We just stopped seeing each other, that's all."

Terrence knew there had to be more to story. "*Why?*"

"Here you go," the bartender brought their drinks and disappeared as quickly as he had come.

"Because," Frank continued over the volume of the bar. "She wanted to." He found himself trying to steal a few glances at the Latino bartender who wore a tight fitting sleeveless t-shirt.

"And you just let it go? Just like that without pushing for more with her? I thought you were more into her than that."

"I don't want more. I mean, I thought I did, but I don't. We're good though—just friends."

"Just friends…" Terrence nodded slowly and looked him in the eyes.

"Mm. Hmm. Just friends."

"Well—" Terrence began, but was distracted by a loud roar coming from another corner of the pool hall where a crowd was gathered around a television showing a boxing match. He soon turned his attention back to Frank. "Um…yeah, well, there's nothing wrong with that."

"What about you?" Frank took this opportunity to change the subject.

"What about me?" Terrence asked with slight defense.

"I haven't seen you with anyone in a long time."

"So."

"So what's the deal?"

"There's no deal. I'm just focusing on myself right now, that and making money and growing my business. That's all."

"T, you're always thinking about money," Frank said and gulped his beer.

"It's the only thing worth chasing. Women get in the way." Terrence finished his drink and pushed the glass away from him. "They're too much drama for me right now."

Just then Yesenia walked in with two other women and positioned themselves at the other end of the bar.

"Yep, some of them can be a pain." Frank noticed Yesenia. "Hey, Terrence, you ready to go?"

"Yeah, just let me close out my tab." Terrence gestured to the bartender to bring the bill.

"Okay, I'll meet you outside."

"All right." Terrence noticed Frank's sudden desire to leave and thought it was odd but decided to let it go for the time being.

Frank downed the rest of his beer and headed toward the exit. He wanted to avoid Yesenia.

Just as he tried to leave, she walked over to him. "Hey Frank, what's your hurry?"

"No hurry, I was already getting ready to leave."

"Why don't you stay?"

"Because I have to go." He was tense. He didn't want to be bothered with being fake with her.

She smiled at him, and paused. "Well, I was just saying hello. It's been a while since we've talked or hung out."

He sighed not knowing what to say next.

She traced the contours of his arm with her index finger, winked at him, and gave him an even broader smile. "I'll see you around, Frank," Yesenia added and left him. She returned to her friends without looking back at him.

Even though he was uncomfortable, Frank tried to be cool and walked out as if he wasn't phased by his run-in with Yesenia. From the bar, Terrence had observed their interaction and was interested in what had happened. He got up and quickly walked toward the door to meet Frank outside.

"Who was that?"

"Just some old business, that's all. I cut her off, but she didn't take it well."

"You never told me about that one. She's fine, man."

"Yeah, but she is the past. I kept it quiet for good reason. I don't really want to talk about her." He was uncomfortable and suddenly wishing he had drunk something stronger than beer.

"Fine, whatever." Terrence chuckled. He was intoxicated and things seemed to be humorous to him for no reason.

"Come on, T, let's get out of here."

Terrence got in the passenger seat of Frank's glossy, black Lincoln Zephyr. Frank had taken it to get detailed earlier that day, and it looked like he'd just driven it off the showroom floor.

"Damn, man what kind of air freshener have you been spraying in here? That shit is strong!"

"Oh, shut your drunken ass up and just relax."

"I'm not drunk," Terrence said with a goofy smile. "It's not my fault your ride smells like funeral flowers."

Frank ignored him and pulled onto the highway.

"Amaaazing grace..." Terrence began to sing!

Frank laughed. "What the fuck, man? Shut up with that shit!"

"All right. Okay. I'll chill," Terrence said and eventually calmed down.

Many thoughts traveled through Frank's mind as he drove to Terrence's house. He was lonely. He needed a vacation. He could use an orgasm. He looked at Terrence. They had been friends for years, longer than he had been friends with Brianna, and the two of them had been spending more time together ever since Terrence had moved back to South Jersey and opened his barbershop. Prior to being an entrepreneur, Terrence had lived in New York for six years, and Frank had only seen him around the holidays if they both happened to be in town. Over the last year, however, Terrence and Frank had become closer friends.

"I need to take a leak," Terrence blurted, interrupting Frank's thoughts.

"Hold it."

"You better let me out unless you want piss on your leather seat."

"You piss on my seat and I'll kick your ass. Shit, man. Hold it, we're almost there."

"Hurry up then, you drive like an old bitch."

"Man, please. You act like a little punk ass kid." He turned the radio up and continued driving.

He was used to Terrence's antics. They'd had the similar sibling-like arguments over and over. They knew each other well, so well that Frank often wondered why he never confessed the real reason he didn't push for more with Brianna or any other woman for that matter. He couldn't say it out loud. Admitting aloud that he felt like a self-loathing homosexual would mean that he had finally acknowledged his desire to have a relationship with a man.

Franklin had never been with a man sexually, but a nagging feeling inside him told him that he was gay. He had known for as long as he could remember, yet never accepted it. He didn't want to. The thought of being a gay man and what that meant to his stature in society was frightening to him. He had spent most of his life moving with the crowd and never going against the grain in order to get where he was. How could he change now? For the longest time, he had been hanging on to threads of hope that he was just bisexual. He was, after all, sexually attracted to Brianna, Yesenia and plenty of other women. There was something that he knew was missing though. Being with women felt more like something he had to do rather than something he wanted to do. Many of his relationships with women were more like simple sexual friendships, and he found himself more attracted and emotionally attached to men. This feeling had been imprisoned since he was a teenager, and he didn't fully understand it. He had been ignoring it.

Anger, depression, and confusion had been stirring in Frank for too long, and he knew he'd have to stop running from himself eventually. He was becoming a powder keg of emotion and would explode if he didn't utter his feelings to someone soon. He was tired of trying to ignore what he felt to be true about himself. *Everywhere you go, there you are.* He'd frequently thought of a statement on a television episode of The Wire and it haunted him. No matter how much he tried to run from his feelings, everywhere he went, there they were.

"It's about time," Terrence said as they pulled in front of his place. He got out of the car and walked quickly toward his condo.

Frank strolled behind him. He was in no hurry at all. He even stopped to take in the beautiful night sky that covered the suburban enclave like a warm quilt. By the time he walked through the front door, Terrence had already used the bathroom and was in the kitchen making a cup of coffee.

"You look depressed. What is the matter with you?" asked Terrence as he pulled a mug from the cabinet.

"Nothing."

"Quit lying, Frank. What's your problem? Want some coffee?"

"No thanks. I just have a lot on my mind, that's all. Anyway, just let me use the bathroom really quick and I'm out of here."

"Go ahead."

Frank left Terrence alone and went to relieve himself. His heart beat inside his chest like a bass drum. He was on edge, full of anxiety. He wanted to tell Terrence what he was feeling but didn't know how. What would happen to their friendship? How would Terrence react? He wanted a friend, an ear, and a soul who would listen and not judge him. Could he trust him?

As Frank washed his hands, he heard sports talk begin to play from the other room. *Relax,* he thought to himself and went back into the living room where Terrence was sitting on the couch watching ESPN.

"I'm going to get out of here. Later, man," said Frank.

"So you're not going to tell me what's up with you?"

Frank thought about it. He actually thought about it. "It's not a big deal. I'm cool."

"Fine, whatever. I'll catch up with you later."

"See you."

Frank stopped short when he reached the front door and turned around to look at Terrence.

"What?" Terrence quizzed.

"I do want to talk, man. I just…" Emotions washed over him. He felt as though he were drowning in them.

"Frank, if you don't stop with this hesitation shit and tell me what your problem is—" Terrence had sobered up. He looked at Frank intently. "What's your issue, man?"

"All right, but you have to understand. It can't leave this room."

"Yes, Frank, just say it. It'll stay here."

Frank paced. "We're cool right? I mean, we're boys so…"

"Yeah, so?"

"So I can be honest with you and it won't be a big deal?'

"Of course, bro. What's up? Whatever it is it can't be that bad. I mean, if your dick is on fire, you can get medicine to cool it down," he teased. "Is that what it is?"

Frank sucked his teeth. "No, man! That's not it."

"I was just playing—trying to lighten the mood. So what's the problem?"

Frank sat down across from Terrence. "Tonight you were asking me all of those questions about Brianna and why I didn't push for more…"

"Yeah."

"There was a reason—"

"I knew there was more to the story! What happened?" Terrence sat up straight.

Frank exhaled slowly before continuing. "Well…I wasn't feeling anything with her. I mean, I care for her. We're friends, but…" Frank was uneasy and started fidgeting with his hands. "I'm tired of having meaningless relationships. I think…I mean I don't think I've been seeing the right people for me to find what I need."

"What are you trying to say, Frank?" Terrence was getting impatient. He ran his hands over his bald head in anticipation. "What are you talking about, dude?"

"All right, I don't know how else to say it, but to just come out with it. I think…" Frank hesitated again.

"Frank! You're killing me, man! Say it!" He threw his hands up in frustration.

"Okay, okay. I—I think I'm gay or bisexual," he said softly and looked down at the floor. He couldn't look Terrence in the eyes. He felt dirty and ashamed.

Terrence turned the television off, sat back, and stared at Frank with wide eyes. He didn't respond right away.

"Well?" Frank tapped his hand nervously. He immediately thought his admission was a big mistake.

"What did you just say?"

Frank was quiet.

There was a piercing silence in the room. Frank's feelings were churning inside him like violent waves at sea. "Come on, man. You know you heard what I said. I don't know. I think so though." The weight of the words tilted inside him, unsure if it should lift or become heavier.

Terrence looked him in the eyes. A smirk appeared on his face. "Yeah, I heard you. I guess I just wanted to be sure you said it. It's okay though. I already knew that, Frank."

"What?"

"What took you so long to admit it?"

"Huh? What do you mean—"

Frank felt a mixture of panic and relief.

"I've had that feeling about you for a while now. I just never brought it up. I didn't know how."

"What do you mean you had a feeling? Do I look gay or something? Do I look soft or like a punk or some shit?" He stood up and stepped back.

"No, Frank! You don't look gay. And what does gay look like anyway? Dude, I recognize the feeling because I know the feeling." Terrence paused and looked at Frank. "I've always been attracted to men."

Eyes widened, Frank studied him in awe. The situation had become too convenient to be true. He didn't believe what he had just heard. As much as he thought he knew Terrence, he had never thought that he might be homosexual.

"Look, I know what you are going through because I went through the same thing when I realized I was gay," Terrence admitted.

"I don't know what to say. I'm ...shit, man. I wasn't prepared for that response!" He was too shocked to be completely relieved at Terrence's revelation. He paced.

"Frank relax."

"You're gay?" His voice softened as Terrence's admission began to sink in. He sat back down, closer to Terrence.

"Yes, Frank. I'm gay. I'm not seeing anyone right now and haven't for a while. Like I told you, I'm focusing on my business right now."

"So..." Frank was at a loss for words.

There was a pause in their conversation before Terrence spoke. "So what?"

"I don't know. How come you never said anything?"

"For the same reasons you're finally just getting around to telling me. It's not the kind of thing you just announce to people."

"Yeah..." Suddenly he began to feel comforted by Terrence's presence. He stared at him. He wanted a hug but was too timid to ask for one.

"So when did you admit it to yourself?" Terrence asked.

"Just within this past year. I always knew, but was never willing to accept it," Frank said.

"Have you slept with a dude before?"

"What? No, man, fuck no!"

"Frank! Calm down." Terrence didn't know if he should be offended or laugh at Frank's convicted response. "Relax, it's me you're talking to. You don't have to be so damned defensive. I just wonder how you can be so sure you're gay if you've never been with a guy."

"Well, I don't know. It's just like I feel like I am not straight. Maybe I'm just curious."

"Maybe."

"I'm attracted to women. I love women, but—"

"Or you might be in phase two." Terrence thought aloud, cutting Frank off.

"What?"

"Most people in the life go through stages of acceptance. First, you deny any homosexuality in you. Then when you can't take that anymore, you settle with being bisexual. Then when you've finally had enough, you admit to being gay." Terrence laughed. "I went through it too."

"You just described me to a T, man." Frank was a little embarrassed at his ignorance on the topic. He looked at Terrence inquisitively. "In the life?"

"Within the community. The gay and lesbian community. It's just a term, that's all."

Their dialog paused. Frank didn't know what to say, and Terrence wanted to leave him to his thoughts. They occasionally glanced at each other or the muted television until Frank broke the silence.

"You know…I really knew that I was attracted to men in under grad. I mean, I knew something was different back in high school. There was this guy named Hector." Frank stared away from Terrence as his mind traveled back in time. A smile began forming on his face at his memory. "He ran track and had the most magnificent body I had ever seen…besides mine," he said and laughed.

"You've got a thing for Latino guys. I saw you checking out the bartender tonight."

"What!?" Frank was embarrassed.

"Relax," Terrence laughed.

"I know, but…"

"It's no big deal, man." Terrence still chuckled at Frank's expense. "What happened with Hector?"

Frank continued his story to avoid the discomfort of Terrence's acknowledgement of his admiration of the bartender. "Hector? I went to his meets but never introduced myself to him. I watched him stretch and run with perfect form and wonderful speed. He took my breath away, but I was sure he was straight, and even if he wasn't, I didn't want to acknowledge what *I* was. Plus, I didn't want to ruin the reputation I had with the ladies and our frat brothers."

"A few frats messed with men."

"For real?"

"Yeah, but it was just a phase for them. They're all straight."

"Wow."

They ended up talking for hours. Frank shared how he'd had several crushes on friends over the years but ignored his feelings. Terrence listened more than he spoke but did take control of the situation when it shifted back to the topic of women.

"Tell me then; what were you doing with Brianna? Does she know? Is that why you two aren't together anymore?" Terrence asked.

"No, Brianna is way too wrapped up in herself to even think anything like that about me."

"Are you sure? I was wondering about her too, wondering if your relationship with her was just a front for both of you."

Frank was surprised at Terrence's admission. He thought about it. "No, I don't think so. She has a one track mind. Work, work, work," he paused to think again. "Brianna?" Frank spoke her name aloud as he mulled over the possibility. "Nah, she's not a lesbian. She's self-absorbed."

"Mm." Terrence listened.

"I couldn't do it with her anymore anyway. Women are just distractions. Most of them don't mean anything to me *except* Brianna. I do love her, just not the way I should if I were straight. I already hurt her once, and I don't want to do it again."

"What do you mean?" Terrence leaned back on the sofa, getting more comfortable.

"I was sleeping with another woman while Bri and I were together. She knew something was up but never found out the details."

"Was it the chick from earlier at the Golden Cue?"

"Yeah, she works for Brianna."

"Damn, Frank, that's foul!"

"I know, man. I know!"

"How do you know this other woman won't tell Brianna? You said she didn't take the break up well."

"We talked about it and she's concerned about how she would look if it came out, so she's going to keep quiet. I really hope she stays with that and doesn't cause any problems."

"For your sake, I hope so too."

"Yeah…" Frank let the conversation about Yesenia dwindle into nothingness.

"So how are you feeling right now?"

"Confused. Relieved. Frustrated. I feel like I'm suffocating. I don't know what to do. I don't want to be gay!"

"Frank, no one decides to be this way. Nobody chooses it, man. It chooses you!" Terrence was annoyed at the ignorance in Frank's words but quickly softened in understanding. His friend was unsure and he needed not be so hard on him. "I'm sorry, Frank. I know it's tough to be where you are right now."

Frank looked embarrassed. "How did you deal with it?"

"I was just like you at first, inundated emotions. I was in denial. I was even suicidal."

"Suicidal?" Franklin was startled by Terrence's admission.

"Yeah, depression. I felt freakish, nasty, and disgusting and even worse after acting on my feelings. It was rough," Terrence said. "My family is better with it now, but when I came out to them, my father disowned me and told me he was taking me out of his will because I was a disgrace to his name." Terrence paused, old pain resurfacing. "He said that if he knew I was going to be a sissy, he would have worn a condom and flushed me down the toilet.

Terrence's story hit Frank hard. He became afraid. What about his family and colleagues? What about Brianna? Would she think he had been sleeping with another man when he was with her, instead of another woman? How would she react?

"I went through a lot of shit, Frank," Terrence continued. "I'll never forget his words. I had to talk to a shrink for a little while to get myself together because I couldn't think of anyone I could tell who would take it well. I wanted to die to get away from it all."

Frank looked at Terrence and listened quietly. They talked for hours until neither of them had the energy to continue. Terrence shared with Frank stories of flings and the one real relationship he had with a man in New York, and how the experience had left him broken and sour on the belief in love.

For two years Terrence had been involved with a man named Jeff. He was similar to Frank in his meticulous attention to detail in everything from his attire to his Porsche, which he rarely drove, to his sleek apartment in Battery Park, Lower Manhattan. Unlike Frank, Jeff had grown up in London and had an English accent that made Terrence melt. A lover of languages, Jeff had also spoken

French and Spanish. He had come to the States on assignment from the bank at which he worked in London to be a part of a group whose goal was to expand their brokerage business in America. He and Terrence had met by chance one summer at a business expo and hit it off immediately as acquaintances, friends, and eventually lovers.

At first sight, Terrence had been struck by Jeff's walnut skin, his charming smile, and the tailored black suit accented by a yellow silk tie. They had dated, traveled the continents, and fell in love. As time went on, however, details in Jeff's stories about his work, family, and background had become inconsistent. When Terrence pried for clarity, Jeff would become upset or evasive, so Terrence would back off. They coasted along for over a year until Jeff said he'd lost his job and fallen on hard times. He had depleted his savings in six months by maintaining his well-to-do lifestyle and expensive habits without an income.

Against his better judgment, Terrence had let Jeff move in with him for a short time until he got back on his feet. Another three months went by, and though Jeff said he'd gotten another job, he hadn't contributed anything to the household. Terrence paid the rent, all utilities, and even Jeff's cell phone bill until, out of frustration, he began rifling through Jeff's belongings and found out that Jeff was not at all who he claimed to be. His name wasn't even Jeff. His passport said *Christopher J. Harper*. He was a liar, a cheat, and a con man, and Terrence was just his latest conquest. Terrence searched Jeff's laptop and found racy e-mails and photos of Jeff with other men and women, a number of them uploaded and captured during the time when he and Jeff were together. Jeff even had a profile on a dating site with *another* alias under which he claimed to be a recording studio executive.

Frank listened intently as Terrence recalled the story of his break-up with Jeff break-up and the drama that followed. Terrence had loved Jeff deeply and was left with a broken heart, new debt, and distaste for love and men. He hadn't been with anyone seriously since then, afraid to make his heart available for pummeling again. As the night pressed on, Frank and Terrence became exhausted. They eventually decided to call it a night. Frank spent the evening in Terrence's guest bedroom.

Rays of sunlight danced through the window of the room the next morning. The condo was quiet, and as he sat up in bed and glance around the room, Frank assumed Terrence was still asleep. The guestroom was plain but comfortable with a contemporary bedroom set and a flat screen television on top of the dresser. The furniture was all black, and the sheets were a mix of black, white, and grey. The closet was open and empty except for a basketball in the corner on the floor.

"Hey, buddy." Terrence peeked his head into the bedroom.

"Hey." Frank was surprised. He hadn't even heard him.

Dressed in striped blue and white pajama bottoms, Terrence walked across the shiny hardwood floor and sat down next to Frank. "You all right?"

"I don't know." Frank was scared. He hadn't felt so unsure of himself and vulnerable since his adolescence.

"Don't worry. It's not the end of the world." Terrence comforted. "You just need time to accept yourself and be at ease with who you are." He gently placed his hand on Frank's shoulder.

Frank swallowed hard, nervous. Anxiety was building inside him like debris being swept off the ground and into a mini-tornado. He could feel each thump of his heartbeat as he slowly reached over and placed his hand on Terrence's thigh but pulled back as if the touch sent an electrical shock through him. They stared at each other.

"Frank…" Terrence began.

"I'm sorry, T." He moved back, lowering his head. Curiosity was shredding him inside.

There was a void in their conversation as they sat contemplating what was happening.

"Let's not do something that we may regret later," Terrence said. "You're curious right now. I don't think I should be the one to be your first."

"Yeah." Terrence was right again.

"Take it slow," said Terrence as he carefully removed his hand from Frank's shoulder. He stood up and took another look at his friend, his eyes gliding down Frank's beautiful dark brown skin and statuesque body. He tried not to let his eyes slip to Frank's lower body, but they did. He could see the impression of Frank's manhood through his boxer-briefs. It was solid and as confident as the morning sun. Terrence tried to ignore the sexual thoughts that were forming in his mind and quickly brought his eyes back to meet Frank's. One thing that he had not told Frank the night before was that he had fantasized about him on numerous occasions. Unbeknownst to Frank, mental images of him had gotten Terrence through more than a few lonely nights.

"Well, I guess I better get dressed," Frank said and climbed out of bed, his sex becoming more evident, pressed against his stomach.

Terrence could feel the heat from Frank's body as they stood only inches apart. His palms and bare feet began to sweat as his mind battled with his body. Despite what he said about not wanting to be Frank's first, his urges were whispering otherwise. He had not slept with anyone in months.

Frank stepped closer to Terrence and hugged him. "Thanks," he said quietly.

"For what?"

"For being a friend."

"Aw, come on now. That's what I'm here for. It's going to be a bit of an emotional roller coaster for you at first, but you can always talk to me," Terrence said and rubbed Frank's back. "Just know that you're not alone and nothing is wrong with you." Stampede. He could feel the blood rushing to his sex as they embraced. He wanted to kiss Frank and comfort him but restrained himself. He stepped back instead. Being chest to chest with Frank was making it hard for him not to advance, but he felt it would be inappropriate.

On his way home, Frank felt as if a weight had been lifted from him.

Chapter 9

Pam was already at the spa and undressing when Brianna entered the changing room. They smiled when they saw each other. Brianna felt a nervous flutter in her stomach.

"I'm glad you made it," Pam said when Brianna had come closer to her.

"Are you kidding? I've been waiting for this experience all week. I've been so stressed out I was counting the minutes until today."

"Well, trust me, you'll feel brand new after your appointment," Pam responded with an attractive grin and calming tone. Clad in only a lace, burgundy bra and panty set, she reached up to retrieve a hair clip from the top shelf of her locker.

Brianna privately admired the details of Pam's body from top to bottom, pausing to take in her sun-kissed skin, shapely curves, muscular calves and neatly polished toes. "I hope so. Thanks again for inviting me," she said before beginning to strip out of her own clothing.

"No problem. Enjoy it." Pam slipped into a white bathrobe and a pair of flip-flops. "I'm going to go in the waiting area and get a cup of tea. I'll see you soon."

"See you."

Brianna quickly finished changing her clothes. There were several other women in the locker room, mostly older than she was, but they were all in their own worlds. She locked up her belongings, put on a robe, and went to the waiting area. As soon as she got there, she began to feel relieved of the strains her campaign had been placing on her. The room was warm and accented by plants and dim lighting. The arched ceiling was painted in shades of brown and green. Faint scents of something sweet floated through the air, and New Age music gracefully poured through the sound system. Brianna had the urge to close her eyes immediately, but resisted.

Pam was flipping through a magazine and sipping tea when Brianna emerged from the changing area. She put the magazine down the moment she saw Brianna.

"Would you care for a cup of tea or a glass of water?" An employee was promptly at Brianna's service.

"Sure, I'll take a glass of water. Thank you," Brianna said and sat down next to Pam.

They chatted until their masseuses called them for their hour of relaxation. In separate rooms, Brianna and Pam were loosened up by the skillful hands of their attendants. Lying on her back, Brianna shut her eyes and let her mind wander to Pam, who in her room, lay on her stomach drifting into a fantasy of her own, which starred Brianna. The masseuses gently awakened the women from their musings when their time was up.

"Ms. Anderson, I'm going to step outside so you can get dressed."

"Thank you," Brianna said placidly. She removed the warm towels from her body and slipped back into her bathrobe and flip-flops before returning to the locker room where she and Pam met back up.

"Are you going to take a shower or do you have to go?" Pam asked. "I know your schedule is tight."

Brianna glanced at a clock on the wall. She did have to leave but didn't want to. She had several meetings to attend. "Unfortunately I have to head out."

"I understand." Pam took off the white robe and let it fall to the floor before reaching for a towel. Her body shimmered from the massage oil. "I'm just going to rinse off really quickly before leaving."

Brianna contemplated her next action. "You know what? I'll do the same. A few more minutes won't wreak havoc on my day." She took off her robe slowly and wrapped herself in a towel, wondering if Pam were looking for opportunities to see her without clothes. Working out three times a week helped keep Brianna's body toned and splendid to the eye. She only stood 5'4" but was height and weight proportionate and had an enticing, ginger-colored body. She wore black, lace undergarments.

In side-by-side shower stalls, Brianna and Pam took brief, but enjoyable warm showers. They got dressed together and promised to catch up by telephone later, and that they *must* do this again! Pam was captivated and sexually aroused when she left the spa. She had found herself closing her eyes and touching herself as she rinsed off, thinking of Brianna. She wanted badly to slip into her neighboring stall and touch her instead.

Not far away at Smith's headquarters, Yesenia walked into the building.

"Hello, can I help you?" an older woman asked. She noticed Yesenia looking around as if needing direction.

"Yes, I'm here to see Colleen Smith."

"And your name is?" The woman pushed her glasses up on her nose.

"My name is Yesenia De La Rosa. She's expecting me."

"All right. I'll see if I can get her for you."

"Thank you."

"No problem." As the woman walked away, her blonde ponytail bobbed in unison with her cottage-cheese thighs. She soon returned and escorted Yesenia to a room where she met with Smith and her campaign manager, Tony. Yesenia had already spoken to Smith over the phone and was interested in the offer Smith had presented.

A few days earlier, Tony had approached Yesenia in a parking lot while she was loading groceries into her car. He had introduced himself and immediately stated that he knew about her situation with Frank. Although he didn't know Frank's name, he knew that she and Brianna were sharing a man. Yesenia was surprised and confused as to how he knew her secret and asked him to explain himself. Tony only responded with a proposition he was hoping she could not refuse.

"I know of a way that you can protect your reputation and get revenge and bolster your career," he stated.

"How?" She took him in, his dark suit, hard white shirt, and blood-red tie made him look like polished scum.

"Take this." He handed her a cell phone.

"What?"

"Talk," he gestured toward the phone.

"Hello?" She spoke cautiously. Suddenly Yesenia wondered if this were some sort of weird attempt to attack her. She tried to think quickly of what she should do if bad judgment had just put her safety in jeopardy. As soon as the thoughts lit up her mind, they were overshadowed by the voice of a woman on the other end of the phone. Yesenia relaxed slightly as she reminded herself that it was the afternoon and in the middle of a bustling parking lot.

Tony listened to her one-sided conversation. Over the phone, Yesenia had scheduled a face-to-face meeting with Smith and Tony to finalize their deal, and Tony left just as casually as he had approached. She went home that night excited for what her future may hold and worried that she would get caught and ruin her name. Nevertheless, she decided to go through with it and meet with Smith. Now here she was at a crossroads in Smith's headquarters.

"So do you think you can come on board?" Smith asked.

Yesenia thought before answering. What if Smith reneged on her promise to give her a spot on the Public Safety Committee? What if she didn't connect her with people who would bolster her career after it was all said and done? This was an opportunity for Yesenia to start to gain power in the community and local government, but she wanted to make sure she was making the right move.

"What assurance do I have that you will keep your word once elected?" Yesenia questioned.

"Why wouldn't I? Yesenia, I take care of my people. You scratch my back and I'll scratch yours. That is how it works in politics. But you fuck me and I'll fuck you like you've never been fucked before." Smith gave a warm smile. "As long as you keep up your end of the bargain and I win, you will be on your way to power and success. This could be the beginning of a long relationship between us."

"Can I think about this overnight?" Yesenia wanted to buy some time.

"No. I need your answer now or we'll find someone else. The election is just under three weeks away. I'm sure you know every day counts. There are at least five other Yesenias in Anderson's camp just waiting for an offer to be made," Smith announced firmly.

Yesenia went over everything in her head, from Frank leaving her for Brianna, to her career as it stood at the moment, to the possibilities of what she could be if she linked up with someone like Smith. She also thought about Smith's ruthlessness and wondered if she would end up entangled in her web. She even considered Smith's chances of defeating Brianna. Yesenia looked Smith in the eyes, "Yes, I'm on board. But if you fuck me, you'll wish you had *only* been fucked back."

Smith smiled at Yesenia's reciprocal candor. She liked this one. "I'll be in touch."

Yesenia stood up and shook Smith's hand and then Tony's. She left with much to ponder. The biggest question was how did Smith know that she and Brianna had romantic relationships with the same man? Yesenia didn't want that to come out in a negative light because it might damage her reputation. It would be best kept a secret forever.

She was going to be involved in a mud slinging countdown to Election Day. Smith had ordered her to find some dirt on Brianna, and she had to do it fast. Now her deal for advancement was dependent on her ability to get closer to Brianna and discreetly feed information to Smith.

"Anderson, where the hell have you been?" Sheldon shouted when he saw Brianna finally walk into her headquarters. He had his hands on his hips, which put his belly on display. His turquoise tie looked just a tad too short.

"What?" Half of her thoughts were still at the spa where she'd spent a pleasant afternoon with Pam.

"Now isn't the time to start fucking up!" Sheldon said matter-of-factly. His deep voice was unwavering.

"Sheldon!" Brianna matched his tension. Though she was aware he had a right to be upset with her, she wanted to remind him that he worked for *her*.

"Look, I don't know what's going on with you, but I know if you don't stop being distracted, you're gonna to get behind. I haven't been busting my ass for the last couple of months for you to go messing up in the final stretch of the race. You have a few weeks left and a lot of work to do!"

"All right! Damn it, I get it! Shit," she paused. *So much for relaxation.* "I'm here now. What do I need to do?" Brianna felt like a child who had just been reprimanded. She sat down at her desk and got to work.

"You need to figure out a way to get some more money so we can do another mass mailing."

"Hey, Shel?" Asad interrupted.

"Yeah?"

"You have a minute? I want to show you something."

"Sure." He turned to Brianna. "I'll be right back, Anderson," he said and walked out.

Not long after Sheldon stepped away did Yesenia appear.

There were three taps on Brianna's door. The sound annoyed her. "Yes?"

"Hey, do you have a minute?" Yesenia said in a sweet voice.

"Not really, but what's up?"

"I wanted to talk to you about the other day in the bathroom," she said, peering down at the floor and then back up at Brianna. She spoke softly and slowly, calculating the amount of vulnerability she wanted to display.

"Don't worry, I haven't told anyone if that's what you're thinking."

"No, I'm sure you didn't. I trust you. I just wanted to say thank you for listening." Yesenia hesitated and then continued. "I'm going through some rough times and don't have many shoulders to lean on. I—I just appreciate your taking the time. That's all." She stopped speaking and waited for Brianna's reaction.

"Don't mention it. You're doing a lot for me. That's the least I can do." Brianna smiled.

"I really admire you for what you're trying to do. I'll work as hard as I need to in order to get you elected." Yesenia returned the grin. "You're what we need in this district, and I feel privileged to work with you." Yesenia paused again, taking a deep breath. "I know you're going to be mayor next and governor eventually. My dream is to be where you are one day."

Brianna smiled. "Is it really?"

"Yes. As a matter of fact, it is," Yesenia confirmed.

"Volunteering on a campaign is a great way to start. You're already on the right track."

"Thank you."

"You're welcome. I've done my share, so trust me when I say it's good preparation."

"Well, you know I was actually wondering something along those lines."

"What's that?" Brianna quizzed.

"Seeing how much influence you've had on the residents on your first campaign, it's obvious that you're someone I could learn a lot from."

Brianna looked at her, waiting for her to continue.

"I wanted to ask if you would be my mentor?"

Brianna was surprised and flattered. She hadn't even won the election, yet she had someone asking her for mentorship. It stroked her ego. "Really?"

"Yes."

"Well," she thought about her answer, "now isn't the best time, Yesenia. The election is only a few weeks away."

Yesenia repositioned, "You won't have to put any extra effort toward me, I promise. All I am asking is just to follow you around and observe and learn. I'll still do everything you need me to do." *Just say yes.*

"How will you continue doing the other activities my campaign needs from you if you're out on the road with me?"

"I'll put in double time and nothing will lapse. It would mean so much to me!" Yesenia's eyes pleaded for an opportunity. She wanted to give just enough emotion to make Brianna sympathetic without making herself look unstable or weak.

In that moment, Yesenia reminded Brianna of herself when she was just starting out and had an eagerness to learn the ropes. If her mentor hadn't been there for her, she wouldn't have met Sheldon, and she may not have been running for council now. Rockville politics was nothing to take lightly. Even on the lowest levels, it was a tough game to learn how to play. Having a mentor was priceless. Brianna decided to give Yesenia the same opportunity she was once given. "Okay." She softened her expression. "When Sheldon comes back, I'll talk to him and he'll get you a copy of my schedule, noting where you can come along."

"Thank you so much! You won't regret this." Yesenia beamed. She was proud of her deceptive maneuver to get closer to Brianna. There was something exhilarating about trespassing on the shady side of Brianna's trust without being detected. She couldn't wait to proceed. Her next step was to get the copy of Brianna's schedule over to Smith right away to tip her off.

The remainder of the day went by quickly. Brianna was exhausted when she finally pulled into her complex that evening. She went inside, tossed her bags aside, and began to make a cup of peach tea. She wished she could call Pam but knew she couldn't. It was on these nights that Frank would have normally come over to keep her company. *Frank.* She missed the wishy-washy comfort of having him around but was happy to not be living a lie. A part of her still wondered who Frank's other woman was, but she shoved it out of her mind. It didn't matter.

Chapter 10

Frank was sitting in his high-backed leather chair in his Philadelphia office with the door closed. He thumbed through a magazine filled with scantily clad men with chiseled bodies. As he followed the contours of one of the model's muscular abs with his eyes, he loosened his tie. He wished he could touch them. He wondered how the model's body would feel pressed against his. He imagined his muscular arms wrapped around him.

His thoughts were interrupted by the voice of his administrative assistant through the intercom. "Frank, I have Terrence on the line for you."

Frank smiled. "Put him through." He picked up the phone on the first ring, "Hey, T."

"Hey, what are you up to tonight?" Terrence asked jovially.

"Nothing, just about to wrap it up here for the day. Are you in the city? Want to get a bite to eat?"

"No, actually I'm at my shop. I was hoping you'd be back on this side of the river by now. What are you still doing in Philly, man?"

"It's been a long one. I've been down to D.C. and back already today."

"Oh, damn," he paused. "Well, give me a ring when you're out of the city. I have a surprise for you."

"What surprise?"

"If I told you, then it wouldn't be much of a surprise, now would it?"

Frank laughed. "All right, fine. I had planned on working out after I left here, so it'll be a little while before I'm home."

"That's cool, dude. I'm around."

"All right, later."

"See ya."

Frank hung up and began to clear his desk, slipping the magazine in his briefcase. He put his jacket on, grabbed his gear and left the office. He was looking forward to going to the gym. Ever since he had admitted his feelings to Terrence, he'd felt a sense of newness about himself that he liked. It was slow revealing itself, the freshness, but little by little the layers of fear that had encrusted his mind began to crack and peel. He still hadn't tested the waters as far as his sexuality but felt comforted to have Terrence as a close friend.

It was late in the evening and Brianna was still plugging away. Franklin had come through for her and got a few more of his friends to donate a total of $5,000 to her campaign. It was just what she needed to buy more pamphlets, flyers, buttons, newspaper ads and the seemingly never ending list of publicity items she needed.

Sheldon, Yesenia, and Brianna were going over how to spend the funds when Brianna's cell phone rang. She wanted to get it but knew she needed to complete what she was doing without interruption.

"I think that's the best way to divvy up the funds," Sheldon said after scribbling allocations down on a sheet of paper. "Spend most of it on the paper ads, pamphlets, and flyers. I think using it for a radio spot is wasteful. You don't need a whole lot of buttons either. "

"If Asad can do the graphic design for all of this stuff it'll save a bundle," Yesenia added. She surprised herself.

"Good idea," Sheldon smiled at her and continued speaking.

Brianna absorbed everything he was saying as he went on to explain the reasons behind his choices. She agreed with it all.

"Yesenia, can you work with Asad to get all of this stuff designed and ordered?" Brianna asked.

"Sure."

"All right. Make sure I see proofs before anything goes to print," she added and stared at her.

"No problem."

"Thanks."

"Anderson?" Sheldon admonished.

"Yes?" She turned her attention to him.

"You should get some sleep. Your fatigue is really showing."

"I'm fine, Shel."

"Are you sure?"

"Of course."

"Okay. I'm just telling you because the next two weeks are going to be draining and tough on you. You have to keep up no matter what though."

"It's nothing I can't handle."

"Good." Sheldon stood up and yawned. "Let's wrap it up. You two need to call it a night."

"You look like *you* need some rest!" Brianna teased.

"Don't you worry about what I need," he said and smiled. "Look, ladies, I'm out of here. I'll see you first thing in the morning."

"See you," Brianna said. She couldn't wait to leave either. Her hormones were raging, and she had found it hard to concentrate for the last hour.

In between her thoughts of work were desires of escaping into a slippery sexual escapade with a woman. What surprised her was the woman in the fantasy was not Pam, but Yesenia. She caught herself paying more attention to Yesenia than she had ever done before. She was attractive—young, but enticing with firm breasts and an alluring backside. She even noticed Yesenia's long eyelashes that curved perfectly over her light brown eyes and her smooth honey oat skin. It had been her youth and obviously the fact that she worked for Brianna that kept Brianna's fantasies at bay, but she did imagine what Yesenia might be like in bed.

Brianna's cell phone beeped, alerting her to new voice mail messages and shocking her out of thoughts. She exhaled. *What the hell am I thinking?* "Excuse me," she said to Yesenia and went to retrieve her phone from her purse.

Losing Control

"Mm hm," Yesenia mumbled. She acted as if she was in her own world, but she was preparing to eavesdrop on Brianna's call.

Yesenia wouldn't get personal information on Brianna so easily, however, as Brianna never returned any calls in front of her staff. All Yesenia could do was subtly watch Brianna as she listened to her voice mail. Whoever left the message made Brianna swoon. Yesenia began to feel anger as she wondered if Brianna was hearing Frank's voice on the other line. She cracked her knuckles and then stretched her fingers to rein in her feelings. She closed her eyes, took a deep breath, and relaxed.

Brianna sent a text message and closed her phone. "You can actually leave now. I'm about to get out of here myself." It was very rare for Brianna to work late without Sheldon around. He wasn't exactly a bodyguard, but she did feel safer with him there on late nights even though a security guard patrolled the parking lot.

"All right. I'll see you tomorrow."

"Good night."

Jealousy went from a simmer to a boil as Yesenia helped Brianna lock up the headquarters. She knew that she was overreacting and too attached to Frank, but she couldn't help herself. She was obsessed with him and, fuck, Brianna didn't deserve him!

Chapter 11

"So what's this surprise of yours?" Frank asked as soon as he settled in at Terrence's place.

"Here." Terrence tossed a colorful shopping bag to him. "I was going to take you to a club but decided against throwing you to the wolves just yet," he said and chuckled.

"Ha, ha, very funny, man. What's this?"

"It's just a little something I thought you could use. Open it up and take a look."

Frank reached in the bag and pulled out two hardcover books. One was a book filled with coming out stories from men of African descent, and the other was a collection of essays on the history of homosexuality in America. He smiled as his eyes passed over the titles and looked up at Terrence. "Thanks, T. You didn't have to."

"Aw, it's nothing, Frank. I hope you have time to actually read them."

"I'll make time." He looked at Terrence fondly. "That was really thoughtful of you. I appreciate it." He put the books neatly back in the shopping bag.

"No problem."

Terrence stared at Frank who was impeccably dressed in an onyx button-down shirt with a matching watch and perfectly fitting, relaxed jeans that fell precisely over his black shoes. One thing he loved about Frank was his tailored wardrobe. Frank always paid

73

attention to detail, rarely missing his weekly appointment at the barbershop. Frank's chocolate body, with broad shoulders and athletic build, was just as well put together as his manner of dress. He walked and talked proudly, with his head up and shoulders back, bestowing the confidence of a god. He was an alpha male whose vulnerability was only now showing when discussing his sexuality. He hid his uneasiness from the world very well and blended in effortlessly.

"So you're not going to take me out?" Frank asked. "Where do you party anyway? I can't remember the last time you mentioned clubbing."

"That's because I haven't been in a while, and when I did go, I had no reason to tell you because well, you know."

"Mm hmm. Well now that everything is out in the open I wouldn't mind going."

"Oh yeah? Wanna go out tonight?"

"Yeah, man. I've been wanting to for a while. I want to see what it's like." Frank was excited.

"I don't even know why I asked that. Of course you do!" Terrence laughed. "Cool, I know of a spot that you might like. The older crowd hangs out there."

"What if I see someone I know?"

"Then he'll have to explain what he's doing there too, that's all."

A look of clarity appeared in Frank's eyes, yet he rubbed his hands together nervously. He wanted badly to go out to a gay club but was extremely paranoid about seeing a familiar face even if it meant the other person was 'in the life,' too.

"What's the matter?" Terrence inquired.

Frank was lost in thought.

"We could go up to New York instead if you want. There are a whole lot more places up there," Terrence continued, assuming he knew what had stalled Frank's excitement.

"Why don't we do that?" Frank asked, visibly relieved by the suggestion.

"No problem."

"All right, cool. Let's go." Frank smiled. He was anxious.

Terrence was amused by him, remembering his own journey into self-awareness and acceptance. "Relax," he said and pat Frank on the back.

"I'm good."

They soon left in Terrence's red, sporty two-seater.

In Old City, Philadelphia, Pam and Eric were having dinner at a swanky seafood restaurant.

Eric noticed that she had been absentminded for the greater part of the evening. "What's up with you?"

"Nothing, baby. I'm fine." She dabbed her mouth with the linen napkin and forced a smile.

He studied her, wondering how long she would lie to him. After 12 years of marriage, he knew when she wasn't telling the truth, and he knew that she was aware of his intuition in this regard. He stared at her, waiting for her to be honest with him.

"What?" Pam was uncomfortable being the target of his penetrating gaze. His hazel eyes probed her, dredging up more uneasiness. She was sad and bored with him but didn't want to admit it. Not yet.

"I'm just wondering where your mind is because it's not here." He took the last bite of his sea bass.

"I'm sorry." She paused. "I don't know. I just feel down I guess," Pam finally finished. She crossed her legs under the table in an effort to stop the nervous tapping of her right foot.

"Why?" He asked.

"I'm not sure."

"Is it me?"

"I don't know." *Is he listening?* Pam wondered. "It could be you. It could be me. It could be work. It could be anything. I just feel a little chaotic I guess."

"Chaotic?" Her word choice surprised him.

"Unorganized. My feelings—I probably just need a vacation to recharge."

Eric listened quietly, hoping to extract more out of her without pressuring her to continue.

"And I'm tired too," she added.

Before he could respond, their waitress came to check on them. "Sir, madam, how is everything?"

"Very good, thank you," Eric responded.

"Would you like another drink?" the waitress asked.

"No, I'm fine, thanks," answered Pam.

"Just a glass of water, please," Eric requested.

"Certainly," the waitress said and walked away.

Pam's eyes followed the waitress for a few seconds before she turned her attention back to Eric. Unaware, Eric wiped his mouth with the napkin and pushed his plate away from him. Pam gazed at him and smiled genuinely.

"What are you smiling at?" Her gesture comforted him.

"You," she giggled. "Am I allowed?"

"Yeah, it just seemed random."

"Well, I don't want to sit here depressed all night."

He grinned and winked at her.

"I think the little talking I just did with you made me feel better."

"Good." He felt relieved. Maybe he needed to take her away for a weekend to unwind.

"Plus, you look really good tonight." Pam tried to get away from the thoughts that were weighing her down. She wouldn't make it through the evening if she dwelled on them, especially in front of Eric. If she had to revert to acting to avoid another uncomfortable conversation with him about her feelings, then that's what she was going to do until she was ready to tell him the truth. She would, eventually. Pam hated to lie.

Eric leaned back and suppressed a smile. He did look handsome in his sky blue shirt and dark slacks.

"Your water, sir," the waitress said upon her return. She cleared their table. "Would you like to see the dessert menu?"

"Sure," Pam answered before Eric.

Ever attentive, the waitress left again and returned with two menus. Eric and Pam ordered and enjoyed sharing a peach vanilla soufflé before leaving the restaurant. Although Pam did become a little less depressed after talking, Eric wanted to put effort into lifting her spirits. He stopped to buy a bouquet of flowers from a street vendor as they walked back to his car.

"Thank you!" Pam responded and covered her mouth in surprise.

Eric had always been romantic. Because he traveled so much, however, she often forgot how thoughtful he could be when he was around. She accepted the flowers and felt a pang of guilt over her lustful desires for Brianna. She kissed him. He pulled her closer and kissed her harder, passionately, holding her tightly in his long arms. She closed her eyes and continued. The longer they kissed, the more it hurt her. Remorse and confusion spun around inside her, ravaging the moment that should have been wholeheartedly affectionate, but she outwardly kept herself together.

Eric was a good man. He was a hard worker, respectful, family-oriented, and handsome. He was tall and slender with vanilla wafer skin, closely cut wavy hair, and a goatee.

"Let's go home," Pam suggested, her voice as soft as a feather.

"Okay."

He slid his arm around her waist, and they strolled back to the garage where he had parked.

Pam's cell phone vibrated in her purse as they crossed the Ben Franklin Bridge, but she ignored it. She peered out of the window at the dark, rippling water below until the movement of her cell phone ceased. She thought it might be Brianna, well, she hoped it was Brianna. *Brianna wouldn't call this late,* she concluded glancing at the time on the dashboard. It was after ten o'clock. She abandoned the fantasy of a friendly phone call from Brianna rescuing her from her evening. Lost in her thoughts, Pam eventually drifted into a light nap for the rest of their short ride home.

At home on her balcony, Brianna sipped a glass of port wine while picking up and putting down her cell phone. She had just finished eating a delicious dinner alone and wanted to call Pam but knew it was too late to do so. They were still tiptoeing around each other. As she watched all the cars crossing the bridge and pouring back into New Jersey after a night in Philly, she became lonelier. She wanted a social life. She wanted a significant other. She wanted a lover, a companion. She slowly sipped her port, savoring the sweet taste as it passed over her tongue and warmed her throat. She wondered if and how she was going to test the boundaries of her newfound friendship with Pam. She knew she shouldn't but knew ignoring her desire would be a goal that was too difficult to reach.

Chapter 12

It was almost five o'clock in the morning when Frank and Terrence decided to call it a night. They had gone from club to club in Greenwich Village, with youthful energy, behaving as if they were in college again.

"Man, I can't believe how many guys are in these clubs!" Frank was beside himself. His own misinformed perception of what most gay men were like was shattered.

"Mm hm. Tons of everyday guys, Frank."

They were both still slightly inebriated but were sobering up as they walked a few blocks to Terrence's car. Frank's mind was flooded with images of beautiful hard-bodied men dancing with each other. He danced with a few after a couple of drinks and prodding from Terrence, wading into the sea of men under the strobe lights and disco balls in the dark, hot clubs. Finally, some of his curiosity and fascination began to give way to satisfaction. A few men even slipped him their phone numbers.

"So how are you feeling?" Terrence asked, although he already knew. He could tell from the smirk plastered on Frank's face, but he asked anyway.

"Indescribable." Frank stuck his hands in his pockets. The early morning air was cool, and a breeze had swept over them. "I feel a lot of things."

Terrence laughed. He was glad that he was able to show Frank a good time and a variety of men.

"It's a whole different world—a subculture that I never even knew existed," Frank added.

"It is, and there is a lot more. I couldn't possibly show you everything in one night, but I'll show you more in time." They also saw some drag queens, which Terrence would have to deconstruct and explain to Frank, who didn't get the point of their flamboyant and sometimes unsightly displays.

They had reached the garage where Terrence's car was parked and waited for the attendant to bring it to them.

"Thanks, T. I had a lot of fun tonight."

Just as Terrence was about to respond, they heard a car horn and saw the attendant pulling the red sports car around the corner. Terrence winked at Frank in response and tossed him the keys. "You drive. You're in better shape than I am."

"No problem," Frank said and slid in the driver's seat.

By the time they crossed into New Jersey, their conversation had quieted somewhat. Old-school soul music funneled through the speakers as Frank merged onto the turnpike south.

"So do you think you're gonna call any of those numbers you got tonight?" Terrence asked as he stared out of the window.

"I don't know, we'll see." Frank laughed nervously.

"Well, whoever gets a call from you will be very lucky." Terrence looked over at Frank and admired his biceps, which protruded through the sleeves of his shirt. "You're beautiful, Frank. Do you know that?" Terrence spoke his thoughts without thinking.

"What? Where did that come from?" He'd never been referred to by that term and blushed in surprise and awkward flattery.

"Just what I said, you're *beautiful,* man," Terrence repeated, looking at Frank more intently. He wanted to touch him.

"Thanks." Frank glanced quickly at Terrence and smiled. He felt a tingle in his stomach.

"I really mean that." Terrence slowly placed his left hand on Frank's thigh.

Frank glanced down and returned his eyes to the highway. "I um…" He wasn't sure how to respond.

Terrence moved his hand closer to Frank's inner thigh and felt his manhood. Neither of them said anything, and only music filled the air with sound. Within moments Frank became full and hard in his clothes. He concentrated on the road, unsure if he wanted Terrence to move his hand away or go further.

Terrence inched closer to Frank, his mind telling him to stop and his body instructing him to unzip Frank's pants. He followed his body and accordingly, Frank merged over to the far right lane. Frank let out a deep moan as he felt Terrence's hand slide into his boxers, gripping him. He wanted him to stop because it was a dangerous distraction from the road. He also wanted Terrence to continue because it was sensational in more ways than one. Still, neither of them had spoken a word as Terrence began to slowly stroke Frank's thick, weighted, pulsating erection.

"T..." Frank said. "I think you should....ahh," his statement was interrupted by a pleasurable moan. He had never felt so stimulated. "Maybe we should pull over. I ..." he stuttered. "I can't drive like this."

Terrence stopped abruptly. "Oh shit, man. I'm sorry. I don't know what I was thinking." He was suddenly embarrassed and removed his hand from Frank's pants.

"Relax," Frank said, trying to calm him. "It's ...it's okay, it's just not safe while I'm going 85 miles an hour."

Terrence looked at him apologetically. He harbored shame for not being able to control his sexual impulse. "I'm sorry." The alcohol was wearing off.

"Don't worry about it," he assured Terrence, shifting his body to zip up his pants.

They rode the rest of the way home without much conversation. Frank had plenty of thoughts darting through his mind while Terrence simultaneously chastised himself and wondered if more would happen between them that night. He thought he and Frank would probably never forge a long-term relationship—he wasn't Frank's type but was curious about the near future. When they finally arrived at Terrence's house, he didn't have to wonder much longer.

Frank pulled Terrence close to him in an embrace and whispered, "Care to finish what you started?"

"You sure?" Terrence responded softly in his ear.

Frank only had a brief hesitation before answering, "I'm sure."

Losing Control

They concluded the evening passionately in Terrence's king bed. Around 9 o'clock in the morning, they finally fell asleep naked and in each other's arms.

Days later, Eric and Pam were at home having a late breakfast when Eric began questioning Pam's attention again. "So are you going to talk to me or what?" he asked and took the last bite of his toast.

"What are you talking about?" Pam dodged the conversation.

"Come on, baby. Do we have to go through that whole routine? You know what I'm talking about. What is up with you lately?"

"Nothing."

Frustrated, he placed his utensils down and stared at her. "Pam," he protested. His voice was coated with irritation.

She sighed and told herself to tell him how she was feeling. Pam and Brianna had shared more conversations and had seen each other casually for lunch over the last two weeks. Their exchange of dialog, glances, and innocent hugs and touches had made it obvious that there was something there. Chemistry. Neither of them said it and they had not slept together, but Pam wanted to explore her feelings for women, and her boredom with Eric was swelling. "You're right, Eric," she answered. "Something is going on and we do need to talk."

He leaned back in his chair and peered at her through unsure eyes. "What is it?"

"Well," she spoke cautiously. "I'm not happy."

"What? Why not? Is it me?" He moved back in closer to her, resting his chin on his fists.

"No, it's not you. You didn't do anything."

"Then what is it?"

"It's me. I'm just not happy right now. I..." she hesitated.

Eric waited for her to speak again.

"I have feelings. Feelings I've always had but have ignored."

He closed his eyes and bit his bottom lip. Uncertainty was already starting to build in him before she had a chance to confess. "Go on."

"A void. An emptiness—feelings of needing something that you can't provide."

"Something I can't provide?" Immediately defensive, Eric ambushed her with questions. "What the hell is that supposed to mean? Are you cheating on me? What's going on, Pam? Is there someone else?"

"Nothing is going on, and no, I'm not cheating on you! Would you let me finish?"

"I'm just saying. What do you mean by that—something I can't provide?" He was pissed at even the thought of him not being enough for her. His ego had taken a blow.

"If you would let me explain, I could tell you. You took my words the wrong way. I'm sorry they came out harsh. I didn't mean for them to. What I was trying to say is that what I feel like I'm missing isn't new."

Many years ago Pam had told Eric that she was attracted to women, but he had told her it was a phase, refusing to believe or give any attention to the subject. She hadn't brought it up to him since then.

"Oh, come on, not this again." He rolled his eyes, knowing what she was getting at.

"Eric!" She threw her fork down against her plate. She thought he would give her more time to express herself.

"I'm sorry. I'm sorry. Go ahead and finish," he said. He crossed his arms against his chest and locked eyes with her. His eyebrows were furrowed and his breathing was deep.

Heavy tears began to form in her eyes. The courage that she had built up to broach the topic with him had been crushed by his dismissal and condescension. She backed away from the table and continued speaking. She wanted to be away from him, yet wanted comfort at the same time. "They didn't go away, Eric. My feelings never went away. They're a part of me and it's getting harder for me to ignore them."

"So who is she?" He asked coldly.

"What?"

"Who is it? I don't think this just came out of nowhere. Someone must have influenced this! What's her name?"

"It doesn't work that way!" *Not completely*. Her feelings were always present, and she had struggled with them in silence for over a decade, sporadically seeking comfort anonymously through message boards and chat rooms on the Internet. Being around Brianna lately did bring them out with force, however. Suddenly what she'd been craving had come within reach of exploration and wasn't such a distant desire.

"So who is it? Have you slept with her yet? Have you been sleeping with women behind my back? I mean what the fuck is all of this shit supposed to mean! Are you bi? Have you been with another man too?" He fired question after question.

"No! You're taking this way too far, Eric. Calm down!" His queries hit her like a wrecking ball. She got up from the table and out of habit, began clearing their places. "What is the matter with you?" she asked. "Since when can't we have a conversation without accusations? Why are you acting like this?"

He huffed and ignored her questions. "You know what? I don't believe this. I don't even want to hear it!" He got up and paced, venting his frustrations with his hands as he spoke. "Why do you want to go and ruin everything we have? Twelve years of marriage and now you're telling me you think you're some lesbian?"

"I'm not *just* telling you!" She protested, her skin getting hot with anger.

"Oh, whatever. This is fucking bullshit!"

"I'm just being honest with you. You wanted to know what was going on with me and I told you!"

"So, do you expect me to roll out a rainbow carpet for you?" he asked with an attitude. "You want a parade or something? A bunch of faggots and freaks in leather shorts and body paint, is that what you want to be a part of?" he yelled with disgust. "I don't want to hear this shit. I've already told you that you are *not* a lesbian! Maybe you're just curious or fascinated or something, but you're not gay! You can forget it!"

"Excuse me? You don't know how I feel. How can you tell me what I am?" She threw a dish in the sink and stormed into their dining room.

"Pam?" he yelled and followed her. "Pamela!" Eric was tired. He had been practically living in hotels for the last two weeks and didn't want to deal with this. He was on edge and was sorry he asked about her feelings because he wasn't ready for her answer. "Pam," he grabbed her by the arm tightly and pulled her close to him. "I'm talking to you!"

"Let go of me!" She tried to snatch her arm away but wasn't strong enough to free herself from his grip. She could feel him breathing on her heavily.

"Have you slept with that bitch, whoever it is that has you all confused?" It seemed as if her instinct to pull away only angered him more. He demanded an answer and grabbed her other arm as she struggled to get away from him. He shoved her against the wall.

Pam's back hit the chair rail, and sent a searing shot of pain through her spine. "Eric, stop it!" He was holding her so tightly she could feel the pressure of each of his fingers wrapped around her arm.

"Have you?" Eric spoke through clenched jaws, and a thick vein was showing on one side of his neck.

In that moment, a sheet of fear covered her. Pam couldn't believe what was happening. Eric had never put his hands on her violently. She didn't recognize him. She didn't see this reaction coming. She became afraid of him. "No," was all she could say. "No." She spoke softly, trying to gather herself under his hold and his questioning.

Eric seemed to transform after she spoke, as if he realized what he was doing. He looked at his hands holding Pam against the wall and then saw the shock and fear in her eyes. His mouth opened slightly as his eyes met hers, and he loosened his grip.

She seized the opportunity and channeled her fear into anger rather than continuing to shrink beneath him. "Let go of me!" This time she pulled away from him successfully. She gained strength. "Don't ever grab me like that again!" She pushed him as hard as she could and moved out of the corner. Her eyes held fire, but behind them were dams that would soon extinguish the flames, leaving her to wallow in the smoldering embers of pain. Eric had severed any thoughts of compassion she thought she might have gotten from him as her husband, her best friend. He had attacked her.

"I'm sorry." He put his hands up to show that he was defenseless. "Baby, I'm sorry. I didn't mean to grab you. I just…" He backed away from her, not knowing what to say. He stared at the carpet rather than look at her. "Oh, Pam, I'm so sorry."

Losing Control

Both of them were silent. The room was hot with tension. Adrenaline was rushing through Pam's blood and sweat was streaming down her body.

Eric took a seat on the couch, tapping his foot nervously and fidgeting with his hands. "Pam, I'm sorry." He stood up almost as soon as he sat down. "Baby…" he walked over to her and reached out, but she backed away.

The tears that Pam had been holding back began to flow, and her moment of rage had vanished. She was so disoriented her hands were shaking. "Stay away from me," she told him. "Get away from me, Eric!" Her eyes burned with sorrow.

Eric stopped in his tracks. "I'm sorry, I—baby, I'm sorry. I don't know what just happened. I didn't mean to." He apologized repeatedly, not knowing what else to say. He was nervous. "Please, baby. I'm sorry." He hoped she didn't call the police! He didn't think she would, but what about the neighbors? What kind of animal had he sounded like? He hoped they weren't as loud as it seemed and that their fight was contained within the walls of their home. Now it was he who was afraid.

Pam didn't respond. She looked at him with tears running from her eyes and ruining her make-up. She said nothing. Any words she could think of were stuck in her throat, tangled in pain. In front of her was a man who could be so loving, she'd never expect him to do anything *but* love her, but he had just demonstrated how he could detest as much as he could love. She never thought his ignorance of homosexuality would manifest itself this way. Twelve years and *this* is what made him use violent force to control her? This was not the man she was used to, and their argument had penetrated her like an icepick.

"Pam, say something, please." He watched as she stood in silence, her hands shaking and eyes absent.

She was lost in her thoughts and walked away from him as if he weren't there. Pam replayed their marriage in her mind as she walked upstairs. She couldn't remember the last time they had had a fight, partly because he was hardly around and partly because she always went along with their routine way of living, never going against what would be predictable. She went inside their master bathroom and locked the door. It was the one place in the house, for some reason, where she always felt comforted.

Cheril N. Clarke

Crouched in a corner, she shed tears caused by the pain of love gone awry. She could taste the salt from her tears as they slid down her cheeks to the edges of her lips. Pam wept silently, trembling in solitude. Despite being enclosed by chocolate-colored walls and gold fixtures, she felt a chill through her body as she replayed the argument in her mind. Despite his words making themselves at home in a dark corner of her mind like a squatter seeking a place to settle, she fought against them. She didn't want to hear his voice in her head. She didn't want to be further lacerated by flashbacks of him manhandling her as if she were deserving of it.

But maybe it was her fault, she thought. It *was* her bringing drama into the relationship with her feelings. Why couldn't she just ignore her desires and go on about her life, which was, as he felt, close to perfection? Would she still be lesbian if she only desired but didn't act on those wants? If she had ignored it for this long couldn't she do it for the rest of her life? Should she? Was her life really almost perfect if, beneath the surface, it was all a lie? Pam didn't know what was right or wrong. Things were coming undone and she was afraid.

Drowning in questions, confusion, and hurt, Pam wanted to forget what had happened. She wanted to undo her decision to tell Eric about her feelings. She closed her eyes and tried to shut everything out. *Breathe,* she told herself and kept her eyes closed. *Breathe.*

Downstairs, Eric paced. He loved Pam. He gave her everything he had and did everything he could to make her happy. He never imagined hurting her like this. He was furious that things had escalated the way they did. Rueful thoughts gathered in his mind like a swarm of bees, and sorrow pierced his heart. He became dizzy with the emotions sweeping over him. How could he hurt Pam? She was his life. He never thought he could do what he had just done. He didn't even know what had come over him or why he had snapped. This wasn't the way they normally handled things.

"Shit," he muttered. He wanted to go upstairs to her but was afraid. He beat himself up in his moment of angry confusion. Eric was ashamed that he couldn't control his temper with Pam and was sorry that he'd grabbed her. She had insulted his manhood. He wondered how she could want a woman. How could she want anyone but him? Wasn't their life happy? Didn't she have all that a woman could want? The only thing that he could not give her was children. They had tried to conceive years ago, but when they were unsuccessful, fertility testing revealed that Eric had a low sperm count. Then, as Pam climbed the career ladder, being childless became an asset, and she had everything else: a beautiful home, a faithful husband, a nice car; he was perplexed as to why she would decide to throw it all away. He went in the kitchen and poured himself a glass of cognac.

Outside, day was fading into night and the house became dim under the evening sky, with only shafts of orange sneaking in through the window. The more he thought, the angrier he became. He threw the glass on the counter, breaking it.

"Fuck!" Now he had to clean up the shattered pieces of glass that had splintered on the counter and floor. He was hurt. He felt powerless. He didn't know what to do or say. He wondered if he might have just given her a reason to leave him, as if she weren't already struggling with the thought. Was he making too big a deal of her admission? He wondered if she wanted help for her feelings and didn't want to leave him? *It could have been that*, he thought. How would it have all played out if he had just listened to her? He blamed himself for traveling so much. He left Pam alone too much! Had he been around more, maybe she wouldn't have even had time to dwell on her old feelings. *Her feelings.* Eric had a hard time digesting and legitimizing Pam's feelings. He thought he could do everything to make her happy and feel fulfilled. He wanted to.

Eric was tired. He sighed and leaned against the counter. The house was still. He couldn't hear her. It was as if everything had just halted except his thoughts. He couldn't stop questioning himself. He tried to think of a way to repair the damage he had just done.

Chapter 13

Time seemed to be traveling faster than Brianna could manage. She had visited two churches, a fire station, and precinct in her district as well as the headquarters for the local electricians' union. Her stomach rumbled as she wrapped up a telephone interview with a reporter from a weekly newspaper.

"I'm aware of everything that's important to the Fifth District residents," she said. "The sewage problem, the poor roads, the vacant buildings and littered lots, the lack of after-school centers for children, I'm aware of it all. I know people are fed up and angry at the possibility of a halfway house being reopened in close proximity to an elementary school." She paused to allow the journalist time to capture all of her words. "And I feel that my plans will make this district cleaner and more pride-worthy than it currently is." She answered a few more questions before ending the call, which had come while she was driving home.

Brianna was grateful for the time alone. Though she was happy to mentor Yesenia, she hadn't yet grown accustomed to having her around so much. It was not easy to ignore beauty.

"Got any change, Miss?" Filthy, old, and dressed in tattered clothing, a homeless man begged loudly, commanding Brianna's attention as she sat in her car waiting for a traffic light to turn green. She rolled down her window and stuck two dollar bills in his grimy hand. Brianna only hoped he wouldn't use it to buy drugs or alcohol.

"Thank you. God bless, God bless!" He said and then kept walking down the median to the next vehicle. "Can anybody help me?"

Just as the light changed from red to green, Brianna heard her cell phone ringing in her purse. She fumbled trying to retrieve it, but was able to grab it before it went to voice mail.

"Brianna Anderson," she answered without looking at the caller ID.

"Hi, Brianna."

"Pam?" It sounded like her, but the voice was so soft Brianna questioned it.

"It's me," Pam confirmed.

"Hi. How are you? Is everything okay?"

Pam took a moment to respond. "Yes. I just…"

"What's up?"

"Well, um. I want to talk to you about something." Pam's voice lacked its normal strength and confidence.

"Sure. What's going on?"

"In person," she added.

"Hm? When?" Brianna was surprised at the request.

"Whenever you can...tonight would be good if you had time. I understand if you don't. I mean…" Pam rambled.

"I do. Is everything all right?" The phone call was sort of alarming. Brianna didn't know what to make of it.

"Not really, and I'm hoping that I can talk to you in confidence. I know this isn't professional and I may even be crossing a line, but I just feel like I can talk to you."

"Sure you can. I'm actually on my way home now."

There was silence on both ends of the phone as Brianna pulled onto the street that led to her building. She slowed down, mirroring the conversation, before speaking again. "Do you want to come over?" She wasn't sure if the question came out right or what *right* was. She wasn't sure of anything at the moment. She'd daydreamed of being at home with Pam plenty of times, but none of her fantasies started like this.

"Can I?" Pam asked cautiously.

"Yeah." Brianna noticed a vehicle behind her and sped up to reach her parking space. An enigmatic tingle tickled her stomach as she got out of her car and walked into her building. She was curious about the story behind this mysterious call from Pam.

The building's security guard waved at her as she passed him on her way to her mailbox. She smiled at him and kept talking to Pam. "I live in the Riverfront Condos."

"By City Hall?" Pam was surprised. Brianna was within walking distance.

"Yes. Do you want to come over now?"

"I can give you time to settle in. I'm still at work and it would only take me five minutes to get over there."

"Okay. Just give me a half an hour and then come over. You can park in any visitor spot. Call to let me know when you're here and I'll meet you downstairs," Brianna said, tucking her mail under her arm. She walked to the elevator bank.

"Are you sure?"

"Of course."

"All right. I'll wait a little while and then come over." Pam's voice was closer to her normal tone and she sounded better than she had at the start of their conversation.

"I'll see you soon."

"See you." Pam hung up and took a deep breath.

The previous day with Eric was still heavy on her heart and mind. She hoped she wasn't making a big mistake by deciding to talk to Brianna about it. She hadn't called the police because she didn't want the drama that went along with it. Pam did love Eric, and though he acted the way he did, she didn't want to see him in handcuffs. Besides the scene it would create for her neighbors and possibly the local media if they got wind of it, the sight of him being hauled away by police would destroy what was left of her heart. To see Eric reduced to such a spectacle would be too much. He was not just her husband, he was her friend. She believed him when he said he was sorry, but she wasn't ready to talk to him yet. Eric had clogged her voice mailboxes at work and on her cell phone, but she hadn't called him back. She hadn't said a word to him since she had told him to stay away from her.

Pam felt weighted down with emotion. She had kept her office door shut for the greater part of the day. She only went to work because she knew that if she'd stayed at home Eric would have too, and she also knew he wouldn't want to make a scene at City Hall. Pam didn't want to be around him and hoped talking to

Brianna would help. A part of her wondered if she should have reached out to a counselor first, but she filed the thought away for later. She wanted to talk to someone who hopefully knew how she felt, not someone whose job it was to listen to her. She counted the minutes until it was time to meet Brianna.

Brianna showered and changed into something more comfortable. She was exhausted and hungry but wanted to know where the evening was going. Something big had to have happened for Pam to call her the way she did. Brianna tried to think of what it might be as she straightened up her place in anticipation of Pam's arrival.

Outside, Yesenia was parked in a visitor space desperately hoping that her hunch to follow Brianna home that evening was not a waste of time and would lead to something. She had not been able to dig up any dirt on Brianna and was getting desperate to find something. She was toying around with her cell phone killing time when Pamela pulled into the parking space right next to hers. Yesenia recognized her as soon as she stepped out of her car. She wasn't sure if Pam might be there to see Brianna or if Pam knew someone else in the building.

Yesenia hoped her attempt at detective work would finally pay off. She knew she couldn't follow Pam inside because it might ignite suspicion, so she waited until Pam entered the building and then pulled another parking space that would allow her to look inside the condo complex through her tinted windshield.

As Yesenia placed her car in the new space, she spied Brianna exiting an elevator to meet Pam. They shook hands and then disappeared into an elevator back up to Brianna's condo, Yesenia assumed. She was intrigued and wondered what kind of shady business Brianna might be up to with the city treasurer. *If it were legitimate, why would Pam look so concerned?* Yesenia wondered to herself. Not long after she lost sight of them, she left and called Smith as she drove home.

"I have new information for you," Yesenia said shortly after they began speaking. She wanted to get right to the point.

"What's that?" Smith asked.

"Anderson and the City Treasurer are connected somehow. They're up to something."

"Pamela Thompson? How do you know?" Smith was immediately intrigued.

"I just saw them together. I saw them shake hands and then Thompson went up to Anderson's condo with her."

"Hmm." Smith took a moment to analyze the information. "We'll have to find out what that's about," she said. "Did you see anything else?"

"No, that's all, but I think something is going on."

"All right. Well, this is a good start. Let me know what else you can dig up."

"I will."

"Good. Listen, I have to take another call," Smith said. "Get back to me on this."

"Sure thing."

"Okay."

They hung up abruptly. Yesenia felt proud of her accomplishment. Smith eagerly wanted to know more about Brianna and the City Treasurer.

At Brianna's condo, she and Pam had settled in.

"Thank you," Pam said. "Thanks for letting me come over."

"Don't worry about it. I just hope I can help." Brianna motioned toward her couch. "Have a seat. Would you like anything to drink?"

"Yes, please. Water is fine, thank you." Pam said and smiled nervously.

"All right." Brianna returned Pam's warm gesture and went into the kitchen to get the drinks.

Alone, Pam glanced around Brianna's condo with its cozy light yellow walls, eccentric lighting, and modern furnishings. The sculptures and vintage art pieces were attention-grabbing and gave her a clue to Brianna's taste.

Brianna soon reentered the living room with two glasses of water. "Here you go," she said, handing one to Pam. She pulled two coasters from their holder and placed them on the coffee table.

"Thank you."

"You're welcome." Brianna sat on down on the couch next to Pam. "So?" She paused, thinking of how to continue. "How are you?"

Pam took a deep breath and sipped her water before continuing. "Well, first I'm actually a little embarrassed to come to you like this. We don't really know each other well but…"

"But what?" Brianna sat back, allowing more room between the two of them. She posted her arm on the back of the couch and looked at Pam. "What made you want to talk to me?"

"I guess I thought that you might understand," Pam responded, wondering if her choice of words was too forward. "You might not be able to relate and if that's the case I'll feel like a big idiot, but I'm hoping that you will." She took another sip of her water and leaned back on the sofa, facing Brianna. Pam tried to relax, but was unsuccessful. Her nervousness was dehydrating her, and the moment of comfort that she had felt while alone with the furniture had evaporated now that it was time to tell her story. She drank more water.

"Maybe I will understand." Brianna picked up where Pam left off. "Are you okay?"

"Not really."

"What's wrong?"

"It's Eric. Well, it's me," she paused. "I don't know where to start."

Brianna touched Pam's knee. "Just start from the beginning," she said softly and removed her hand. "Take your time, it's okay."

In that instant, Pam felt a little relieved. She felt safer. She took a deep breath and began speaking. "The beginning, huh?" She smiled sadly and continued. "Well, Eric and I had a fight. A big fight."

"Why? About what?"

"About us, about me—our marriage." Pam hesitated.

"Don't worry," Brianna assured. "Whatever you say here will stay with me." She could feel that Pam was still afraid to confide in her.

"It has to."

"It will."

"If anything from this conversation ever came out, I would deny it all."

"Pam," said Brianna as she tried to give a comforting smile, "I won't say anything. Trust me."

Pam didn't want to offend Brianna, but she had to remind her that she expected confidence. "All right," she finally said.

"So what's wrong with your marriage?"

"It's…" Pam searched for words. "It just can't work much longer with the way I feel."

"What do you mean?"

"I mean I do love Eric," Pam answered instantly, almost as a continuation of her previous statement rather than a response to Brianna. "But I also feel incomplete and unfulfilled."

"Is this new? The way you feel? Is it because he travels a lot that you're not happy?"

"No, it's not new and it's actually not even him." Pam tapped her foot in nervousness. Shoulders slumped over, she stared at the floor. She felt tears welling up, but didn't want them to fall. She felt weak but didn't want it to show. She looked up at Brianna.

Brianna looked back at her, and Pam stalled.

"He's a good man. He does everything for me even when I tell him he doesn't have to. I feel guilty for not being happy with him."

"Guilty?" Brianna thought it was a heavy word to describe her feelings.

"In a way, yes. I *should* be happy, but I'm not. He's so upset right now. I can tell he doesn't know what to do. He doesn't want us to end."

Brianna listened as Pam continued to talk in what seemed like random statements. She was waiting for Pam to tell her exactly *why* she was unhappy, but Pam didn't volunteer the information. She talked more about Eric than herself.

"Are you saying that *you* want a divorce?" Brianna probed.

"I don't know. Ultimately, I guess so."

"Okay. Let's back up. What made you two get into the argument in the first place?"

"Eric. He's noticed changes in my behavior and started asking me what was going on," Pam answered. "That's how it started. I had to tell him something and didn't want to lie to him, so I told him the truth."

"What's the truth?"

A single tear began to slide from Pam's right eye. A wave of anxiety washed over her as she thought about answering. She leaned back into the sofa and lowered her head again. More tears soon followed. She was too choked up to speak anymore.

Brianna extended her arms to Pam for a hug. "Hey, come here."

Pam timidly glanced at Brianna.

"It's okay. Whatever it is, it's okay." Brianna said. She was moved by Pam's raw display of emotion and had to control her reaction. Pam's crying chipped away at Brianna's buried feelings of self-denial.

Pam moved in to accept Brianna's hug, finding solace in the embrace. Brianna comforted Pam quietly as similar feelings stirred in both of them. Pam had wanted to talk to another lesbian for so long; the feelings had been building into a tsunami inside of her, towering on the verge of destruction. It was a difficult moment. Pam exhaled loudly and Brianna rubbed her back.

"It's okay," Brianna whispered.

Pam inched closer, making their hug tighter. She could smell Brianna's hair and feel the warmth of her breath on her ear as she whispered consolation. Pam closed her eyes. Immersed in the moment, she planted a soft, slow kiss on Brianna's neck.

The gesture caught Brianna off guard. It launched a tingle up her spine and a hard pulse in between her legs. She eased out of the embrace and kissed Pam on the lips. Pam kissed her back and they continued with closed eyes for a few moments before stopping and staring at each other. A million thoughts rushed through both of their minds. The condo was completely silent after their kiss. Pam's heartbeat sped up as worry rushed through her at a dizzying pace. She wiped the remnants of her tears from her eyes.

Brianna reached for a box of tissues that was on the end table closest to her and gave it to Pam. She wasn't sure what to say. The moment was tender, and she wanted to handle it with care, but she also wanted more.

In the awkward silence, Pam smiled. She felt embarrassed and afraid, yet her reaction was a smile. She had finally gotten a taste of Brianna, and though sweet, it was sprinkled with sadness due to the circumstances. She felt conflicted.

"So…" Brianna was still at a loss for words.

"I guess that hints at the truth," Pam whispered.

"What?" It hadn't struck Brianna that Pam was picking up their earlier conversation about the argument with Eric.

"The reason why I'm not fulfilled by Eric…is because I'm attracted to women."

Brianna was silent. She was relieved to hear Pam finally reveal the truth. She wanted to confess that she'd been enchanted by Pam since the moment they had met, and she too, was attracted to women. She didn't respond immediately though. Her thoughts consumed her.

"Are you going to say anything?" Pam was nervous and anxious for Brianna to acknowledge her confession.

"I'm sorry," Brianna said and then smiled. "I guess I just veered off into a bit of deep thought."

"Well?" Pam peered at her through eager eyes. Sad eyes.

"I do understand how you feel, Pam. I feel the same way. I have always been drawn to women. I've um," Brianna debated her words. "I've actually been attracted to *you* since the day we shook hands."

"I remember that moment, the handshake. Ever since then I've been wondering what exactly has been going through your mind."

Brianna chuckled lightly. "A *lot* of things have gone through my mind." She gazed at Pam with endearing eyes. "I've been enthralled by you to be honest." She reached for her glass of water and took a sip. She was trying to be careful about how much she divulged.

"Enthralled?" Pam was flattered.

"Very much," Brianna answered. "It's been hard to hide it." She cleared her throat, sat back, and tried to tread lightly in her conversation.

"Same here," Pam said and winked.

Their continuing conversation uncovered bits and pieces of their history, curved and colorful like the hues of a rainbow. Brianna's curiosity led them back to a discussion about Eric and Pam's rocky marriage.

"Can I ask you something?" Brianna looked Pam in the eyes.

"Sure."

"Have you been with another woman before or have you just had the desires to?"

"I've been with women before," Pam answered, "y*ears* ago, before I married Eric."

"Why did you marry him?"

"Because I *wanted* to be straight. I didn't want to be gay. I didn't want to accept my feelings."

"Mm," Brianna acknowledged quietly and continued to listen.

"I was raised under strict Christian faith, and as far as I knew being homosexual was a sin," Pam said, the tone of her voice fading to a depressed grey. "My father is a preacher and that didn't help."

"Oh, wow." Unlike Pam, Brianna never had any type of religious struggle. She was not religious at all.

"Yeah—although there are a lot of things that are a sin…" Pam paused. "I just didn't want to add another layer of struggle to my life if I didn't have to. But I guess I do have to because I can't run from who I am."

Brianna didn't want to open up a conversation on religion and homosexuality. Not at the moment. It would be too exhausting. She navigated away from the subject.

"Did Eric know that you desired women when he married you?"

"Yes. He dismissed it as a phase. I think he's just been in denial about the whole thing. Unfortunately, I've helped him by burying that part of me."

"He was probably hoping it was simply a phase because he didn't want to lose you. He loves you."

"I'm sure he was and I know that he loves me, but where does that leave him and me now?"

"I don't know."

Pam became teary-eyed again. "It's hard for me to remember my life without him. It's not easy to just walk away."

"I understand."

"Especially into the unknown. I know Eric. I know what life with him is like." *What about the fight? Did you know that?* Her memory jabbed her. *At least I thought I did.*

As the evening wore on and their hill-and-valley conversation reached its final lull, Pam prepared to leave. She was exhausted after having touched every color on the spectrum of emotion within 24 hours. It was time for her to go home. *Home,* she thought and wondered how that would go. She had not spoken to Eric since the previous evening.

"Brianna, thank you so much for letting me come over." She touched Brianna's hand.

"You're welcome," Brianna responded with a pleasant smile. She took Pam's fingers in her palm and rubbed her forearm with her other hand. "You can call me anytime," she said. "Let me know how things go."

"I will. Thank you."

Brianna ran her index finger up the center of Pam's arm and gently touched her biceps, traveling farther up. She squeezed Pam's shoulder carefully. Her mind told her to stop, but she ignored it.

"I should go," Pam said, halting the moment. Guilt and intrigue, shame and elation, stimulation and fear flurried all about inside her. She *had* to leave.

"Okay."

Pam stood up and Brianna followed suit. They shared a glance before Brianna began to walk toward the door to lead Pam out.

"Get home safely," Brianna said and moved closer to Pam for a hug.

Pam stepped into the embrace and they held each other silently. Pam sniffled, still reeling from scattered emotions whirling inside of her. "I'm not looking forward to going home." Her voice was hushed. She was tired.

Brianna rubbed Pam's back to soothe her. "I know, but don't worry. It'll be okay." Brianna eased out of their hug, her lips grazing Pam's neck, badly wanting to kiss her again.

Not ready to let go, Pam pulled Brianna back to her. Feeding on desire rather than logic, Brianna became weak and kissed Pam delicately on her cheek, the tip of her tongue tasting Pam's skin.

Heat ran through Brianna as Pam sighed heavily in a pleasurable but tainted response.

"I'm sorry," Brianna said. She was disappointed that she hadn't exercised more control.

"It's all right." Pam let go of Brianna and they locked eyes. She then kissed her deeply on the lips.

Their breathing accelerated. Pam backed up against the door and pulled Brianna closer to her. They kissed full, hard, and long, all while letting their hands wander onto each other's body. Brianna felt shivers inside. The continued contact with Pam's tongue and lips incited a warm liquidity in between Brianna's legs. Her muscles tightened in excitement as ecstatic sensations awakened in her body during their kiss. The intensity that came along with satisfying this desire was mind-staggering. She and Pam were exchanging energy, building it with each second.

When they stopped, they looked at each in quiet wonder. Frozen in the moment, it took a few seconds for Pam to make a sound. A moan was all she could muster as she stood there with sexual tension radiating inside of her.

Brianna's ringing telephone broke their moment.

"I have to go," Pam said again. She looked afraid. "Um. I'll call you."

Shit. I hope I don't regret this, Brianna thought, noticing the expression on Pam's face. The phone continued to ring but Brianna ignored it. "All right."

"Good night."

"Night." Brianna opened the door for Pam and watched her leave. Pam glanced back at her before entering the elevator and then she stepped inside. When Pam disappeared, Brianna closed her door and leaned against it while replaying the evening in her mind. *Reality never goes as smoothly as fantasies.* She had no idea how things were going to play out with Pam now. Pam could decide she wanted to stay with Eric because he was familiar. She could do that and ignore her desires or do it *and* try to explore with Brianna. The latter went against a personal rule that Brianna had never broken: Stay away from married people.

She wanted Pam, but not at any cost. As she walked to her kitchen, she thought about the additional pressure that she would face by sneaking around with a married woman. Not only was that act of adultery morally wrong, it would wreak havoc on her career if someone found out about them. She wasn't sure she could handle the consequences of treading the dangerous waters of an affair. What would people say about her character and her integrity if the truth got out to the public? It could kill her career before it had a chance to flourish.

"Damn it," she thought aloud. They had already trespassed on the other side of morality when they kissed! *She's married!* Brianna chastised herself, but how could she ignore her desire, dismiss their kiss, and go on as if it never happened? She trembled at the sweet taste of Pam's tongue sliding into her mouth for a sensual dance with her own. Brianna didn't, however, want to be poisoned for knowingly partaking in forbidden fruit.

Her telephone rang again, calling her attention. She reached for the cordless unit on the kitchen counter and saw from the ID that it was Frank. She debated letting the call go to voice mail but decided he might be a good distraction from the thoughts that were running wild in her mind.

She answered. "Hello?"

"Hey."

"Frank, how are you?"

"I'm good. I was just thinking of you and I thought that we hadn't spoken in a while."

"I know. I'm sorry."

"Don't be. I've seen you on TV. I know you're caught up with the race."

"Yeah, it's down to the wire now. To tell the truth, I'll be glad when it's over."

"Tired?" he asked, already knowing the answer.

"Exhausted."

Frank smiled to himself. It felt good to talk to Brianna again. Although it had only been a few weeks since the nature of their relationship had changed, it felt much longer to him. Her voice comforted him in a way that was contradictory and uncomfortable. "You can do it," he said. "You're strong and you're smart. I believe you're gonna win, and when you do, all of the work you've done will have been worth it."

"Thanks, Frank."

"Mm hm. Hey, do you want to go grab a bite to eat?"

"What?"

"Eat. Dinner. Food, you know—fuel for the body?" He laughed and continued. "But not like a date, just dinner as friends."

"Tonight?"

"Yeah, I mean if you've already eaten then no, I guess, but I'm starving and just thought we could catch up a bit like old times."

"Like old times, huh? All right, why not? I *am* hungry."

"Cool."

Frank was happy that Brianna said yes. His personal journey into self-definition wasn't a horrible experience, it was a confusing one no less. Though he claimed he wasn't asking for a date, a part of him felt that he was going out with Brianna give him a sense of normalcy. As engaged as he was by men and his experiences with Terrence—they had had sex again—he wanted to feel normal—*heterosexual*. At least that was the only definition of normal that he had ever known. "Do you want to pick the restaurant?" he asked.

"You can choose." Brianna walked into her bedroom to change clothes. "Some place casual though. I don't feel like getting all dressed up." She then paused, thinking that though this wasn't supposed to be a date, it sounded like one. But then she thought that she was reading too much into it. She and Frank used to go out all the time before they started sleeping together. *Old times.*

"Well then let's just go to T.G.I. Friday's."

"Hmm. How about going to a private restaurant instead of one of the chains?" she countered.

"That's fine."

They finally decided on Christo's an old hole-in-the-wall Greek joint they enjoyed. Brianna slipped into a pair of fitted jeans, a biscuit brown sweater, and heels. As she applied her make-up and put on her jewelry, she wondered why she accepted Frank's invitation and why he extended it in the first place. It was true that they used to hang out all the time, but something felt different that evening. Nevertheless, she'd agreed and was expecting him to arrive to pick her up shortly. She thought about Pam, wondering if she and Eric were talking right now. Brianna was curious as to how their conversation might be going and what the outcome was going to be. She wondered when she would speak to Pam again and how *their* meeting would go. The more questions popped up in her mind, the happier she was that she was meeting with Frank.

Chapter 14

In Cherry Hill, while Frank ran his hands over his face to check if his shave was perfect, Yesenia was parked in a visitor's spot at his residence. After leaving Brianna's, she had gone home but ventured back out and found herself driving to Frank's to see what he was up to. Yesenia ended up parked a few spaces down from his car, in between an SUV and a tan minivan. She could see people going in and out of the building without being noticed so long as she remained sandwiched between the two big vehicles.

While Frank was upstairs spraying on his cologne and putting on his jewelry, Yesenia was downstairs thinking that once she helped Smith get Brianna out of the way, *she* would become powerful. She could become his significant other just like Brianna, but better. In her delusional fantasy, she would get a career boost and win Frank, and Brianna would be irrelevant. She smiled at the thought.

Moments later she saw Frank strolling out of the building looking dashing as usual. Just the sight of him jarred her memory. She could taste his kiss, smell his body, and feel the strength of his thrusts inside of her on their sexual escapades. They could be perfect together were it not for his distraction with Brianna. Yesenia watched as he pulled out of his parking space. Soon after, she started her car and followed him from a distance. Her recollection of their bold adventures was marred when she realized from the route that he was taking that she was heading right back to Brianna's place. The confirmation of her enemy entertaining her man upset her. Yesenia became furious as she watched Brianna smilingly get into his car, neither of them paying attention to their surroundings and clueless to her presence.

"You just wait, Brianna," she vowed as she followed them to the restaurant. "You think you have him, but you don't!"

Yesenia found a corner parking space far away from Frank's, waited twenty minutes to give them time to be seated, and then went inside. Finding a seat at the bar where she could steal glances at them, she ordered a Kamikaze and an appetizer to further blend in with other bar patrons. But she could only take so much of seeing Brianna and Frank laugh and talk with each other before she decided to wait outside. She hated seeing them together but couldn't convince herself to go home and abandon her actions. Rather, she dreamed up entire scenarios as she sat in her car. She waited a half an hour for them to emerge and was trying to talk herself into leaving, when she saw them exit. She stayed.

Frank and Brianna came out of the restaurant gabbing and smiling, looking as if they'd just had a blissful date. They saw a familiar face as they walked on.

"Terrence, hey!" Brianna exclaimed when she saw him.

He looked surprised to see her. He was, especially with Frank on her arm. "Brianna, Frank, hey, what's up!" He flashed a smile and stared at Frank.

"What's up, T?" Frank could see the shock in Terrence's eyes.

Yesenia got out of her car and walked to the side of the building so she could hear their exchange better.

"Not much. I was just running to the cash machine is all. How are you two?"

"Pretty good, just decided to go out to eat for a break from campaigning," Brianna answered.

"Yeah, just eats, that's all."

"Cool." Terrence said. "Bri, can you excuse us for a sec?"

"Sure."

It was obvious to Frank that Terrence was bothered by seeing him with Brianna and figured he would have to smooth things out with Terrence quickly. He wished Terrence would have just made small talk and left, but he didn't, and now Frank felt uncomfortable. They walked a few feet towards the unexposed Yesenia. From her position, she was able to hear them much better than Brianna could.

"Terrence, what's up, man?"

"Nothing," he lied.

"Come on, dude. Why do you look upset? We're just having dinner. It's not a date."

Terrence pouted. "It looked like one."

"You got the wrong impression. Anyway, can you just chill? She and I are just hanging out the way we used to."

Though they were whispering, Terrence's words grew louder than Frank's and were weighted with enough jealousy that even he was surprised. "I thought you said you guys weren't seeing each other anymore. That's what you said the other night."

"We aren't."

What? Yesenia was trying to make sense of their exchange.

Terrence questioned Frank's response with a sharp gaze.

"I said we weren't sleeping together anymore. I didn't say we stopped talking to each other all together. We're still friends, man."

Terrence gathered himself. "All right, Frank. My fault. I don't even know what got into me. I'm sorry for overreacting."

"Don't sweat it. Just be cool. Chill." Frank had never seen this side of Terrence. He wasn't sure if he should be flattered or paranoid or take it as a warning sign of possessiveness.

Frank and Terrence were not in a relationship but it was obvious that Terrence's feelings were becoming territorial. Maybe it was simply because Frank was with a woman instead of a man. Terrence had made no secret that he did not date bisexuals, but that affirmation was challenged after sleeping with Frank. Complicating the situation more was that Terrence's fondness for Brianna as a friend. He was embarrassed that he couldn't restrain his feelings in front of her and hoped he didn't arouse suspicion where there hadn't been any. Frank would not take that lightly.

A few feet away, Brianna watched their exchange. Although she couldn't hear them well, she could tell from their body language that something wasn't right. She had to question herself when she wondered if Frank and Terrence were having a lover's quarrel. *Lover's quarrel?* No way, but that's what it looked like.

Around the corner, Yesenia stood in utter surprise as she listened to Terrence and Frank. She covered her mouth, which had opened in surprise as she strained to hear all of their words.

"I'll call you when I get home," Frank said.

"You don't have to. I mean, you don't have to if you weren't already planning to."

"Terry!"

Terrence looked at Frank. The nickname softened him. Frank had never called him that before, but it felt good to hear. Frank gave him a charming smile and didn't have to say anything else.

"Okay," Terrence said and grinned. He relaxed.

"Come on, you have to say good night to Bri," Frank said. He began walking and Terrence followed.

Hands in pockets, Terrence walked behind Frank hoping he didn't come off as bitchy as he thought. As they walked back to Brianna, Frank felt a bit overwhelmed. Had he left her alone too long? Had she heard them? Was she upset? Fuck! When they reached Brianna, Terrence smiled politely.

"You guys all right?" she asked.

"Yeah," they answered simultaneously.

The following silence in their conversation negated the answers the men gave.

"Okay," Brianna said. She would ask Frank again when she was alone with him.

Terrence glanced at his watch. "Well, it was good to see you two. I do have to run though."

"All right, T. I'll catch up with you later."

"Good night, Terrence," Brianna added.

"Good night." Terrence grinned at them both. He gave Brianna a hug. "Take care."

Terrence wanted to hug Frank too, but Frank didn't budge. He reached out for a handshake instead, which Terrence accepted, and they embraced in a less intimate, one-handed masculine way before going their separate ways. Terrence walked in the direction of the ATM. Yesenia waited where she was until all three of them were farther away before she walked gingerly back to her car. She was too stunned to streamline her thoughts and assess everything she'd just taken in.

Brianna couldn't wait. "What was that about?" She quizzed Frank as they walked to his car.

"Everything is cool, Bri. We were just talking."

"It looked like more than that, Frank." She wasn't letting up. She wanted to know the truth.

Frank didn't answer her immediately. Brianna wasn't stupid and must have read into what she had seen. Frank was chilled by the thought of Brianna suspecting him. He didn't want to insult her intelligence by lying, but he sure as hell didn't want to tell the truth either. They got into his car.

"We just had a little misunderstanding," he said as he started the ignition and pushed the button to activate his personalized seat and mirror settings.

Every silent second felt lengthened as Frank hoped Brianna would drop the subject. He swallowed hard, uncomfortably nervous at what could be his first coming out experience since Terrence. Though he tried to act cool, he was full of anxiety. He wasn't ready to tell her or anyone else for that matter.

"Frank?" She looked at him, noticing the discomfort that was draped over his every movement and seated in his eyes. "What happened back there between you and Terrence?" She wondered how she would react if he confirmed that it *was* a lover's quarrel.

"Bri, I told you."

"You didn't tell me the whole truth," she said. "You *owe* me that much." Her voice was tinged with hurt.

Ouch. He pulled onto the road. *What was that supposed to mean? Was it a jab at him for their never-settled phone-call incident? Did she now think it might have been Terrence and not a woman?* Oh, fuck! The last thing he wanted was to be thought of as some "down-low" guy. Still, Frank was confused. She was not upset and was speaking at a normal level, which was odd if she thought something was going on with him and Terrence.

"All right. It was more than that," he said, not taking his eyes off the road.

"Are you going to tell me what it was about?"

He grunted and took a deep breath. "I don't know what to tell you."

"Just be honest with me, Franklin. Is there something going on with you and Terrence?" she asked. She didn't want to skirt around the issue any longer.

Frank's mouth was dry, his hands were sweaty, and his heartbeat began to pick up speed. He couldn't answer her. The words wouldn't come out. Brianna looked at him with wonder as he slowed to a stop at a red light. Frank tapped the steering wheel nervously, unable to look her in the eyes. A knot was forming in his stomach. Shame and fear raced inside of him, kicking up a cloud of emotional dust.

"Frank?" Brianna called, the pitch of her voice rising in realization that his lack of a response was, in itself, an answer. Suddenly she became uncomfortable. She felt hurt. "Are you and Terrence in a relationship?" The words almost choked her as she spoke them. Had she been that blind? Was it true?

There was enough tension building in the car to smother them both. Frank didn't say a word.

"Frank!"

"What?"

"Answer me!"

"I can't."

"So you *are* in a relationship with him?" Her stomach hit the floor.

"No, I'm not!"

"Then what is it?" She pushed.

Frank swallowed hard. His feelings were running wildly inside of him as if trapped in a dark jungle.

"Have you slept with him? Is that it?" She couldn't take it anymore. She wanted him to come out and say it!

"Yes," Frank finally said. He spoke softly. He was getting a headache. He wanted life to halt, just pause for a moment for him to catch up with it.

They had arrived at her condo and he still couldn't look at her. He hung his head, feeling like a timid child rather than a grown man. He could not find any more words to say as stress began to lodge in his throat. Worry and vulnerability consumed him.

Brianna didn't know how to feel. She was angry, but she wasn't sure at what exactly. She was perplexed. Why didn't she already know this? Was she that absorbed in herself or was he just good at hiding it? Was he gay or was he bi? What in the blue fuck was going on?

She touched his shoulder, tears forming in her eyes without notice. Brianna began to feel sadness. "Why don't you come upstairs?" she asked. Frank was a reflection of her and if she was angry at him, then she was ultimately angry at herself. Her thoughts were numbing.

"What?" He was surprised. Finally, he looked at her.

"Come up with me so we can talk."

"What's going through your mind, Bri?"

"Questions," she said, "thoughts and more questions. A lot is going through my mind, Frank. I can't even say them all out loud because they're not organized. It's a just a collision of my heart, my mind, and the truth." She opened her door. "Come on. I need to talk to you."

He bit his bottom lip and turned off the car. "All right, let's go up." The air between them was thick with apprehension. They got out of the vehicle and went upstairs to her condo.

Yesenia had finally decided to stop following them. She had observed enough and couldn't stomach the thought of camping outside of Brianna's place. She went home. Frank was a faggot! Her head was ablaze with condemnation, confusion, and anger. She didn't know how to handle this new information. Did Brianna know or was she just as surprised? No, if she knew about Frank, why would he walk away to talk to the other man? *The other man!* Yesenia wanted to vomit at the thought. She was disgusted by it. Frank was a homo, a fudge-packing nasty gay! What if he had AIDS and had exposed her to it? She panicked, trying to sort through her thoughts until she was too tired to dwell on them anymore. Eventually she fell sleep fully dressed.

Brianna continued to question Frank as they sat on her couch. She wanted to know how long he and Terrence had been sleeping together and if it were Terrence who phoned Frank that night their physical relationship took a silent turn towards its demise.

"No," he answered immediately and firmly. "That wasn't Terrence."

She paused, hurt even more to think that there was *another* person in Frank's world. Brianna wanted to know who the other person was but thought that remaining ignorant might be less painful. She resisted her urge to question him more despite the way it ate her up inside to concede. She closed her eyes and took a deep breath. The jealousy made her sick.

Frank was grateful that Brianna didn't press him for more details. He went on to tell her the timeline of his dealings with Terrence. "He and I weren't involved like that at that time," Frank explained. "And he's the only man I've ever slept with." He thought it would soften the blow if she knew it was another woman rather than a man. He was grateful that at least *that* part was true.

Frank told himself that if he could, he would keep his fling with Yesenia a secret until he died. If Brianna found out, their friendship might be irreparable. From her immediate reaction about Terrence, Frank believed he could repair his relationship with Brianna. She didn't yell, curse, or give him any drama. She listened and asked him questions instead. He didn't like lying to her but had to about Yesenia. There was no need to be too honest. That was his burden to carry, not Brianna's.

"Why didn't you tell me before, Frank?" She already knew the answer, but the question was natural.

"Are you kidding? How could I? I didn't know how you would react. I didn't want to scare you and I didn't want to lose you. I didn't want to lose you," he repeated as he looked into her eyes. "I love you, Brianna."

"You love me?" *What a stupid question.*

"Yes, I do. I have for a long time. At first it was just as a friend, but when we started sleeping together, defining what kind of love it was got harder."

Brianna didn't respond.

"I still don't know how to define it."

Brianna listened to him while guilt built up inside her for not admitting how she felt. It was the perfect opportunity, yet she stalled in taking advantage of it. Now was the time to do what they should have done in the beginning: talk to each other honestly, define their relationship, and establish an open atmosphere in which they could both feel comfortable being themselves. She leaned back on the sofa and rubbed her forehead. *Talk to him. Tell him.* She tried to find the words to come clean.

"Bri?" He touched her leg and inched closer to her. "You have to understand why I didn't say anything about my feelings—the gay ones."

She looked at him. "Yeah, Frank, I do."

"I'm glad." His body language confirmed his words and his heart rate had slowed. Frank's nerves had calmed. "Do you love me?"

"Hm?" She was deep in thought.

"I said, did you or do you love me, Bri?"

She shook her head slowly. "Yes. I do love you, Franklin." Her feelings were seeing the light of day. "I'm a little overwhelmed right now."

"I know it's a lot to take in."

You only know half of it, she thought. "I was hurt when I found out there was someone else in your life. I was jealous, but I never said anything about it because we weren't a couple so I had no right."

"You can't control what you feel," Frank said. "I'm really sorry I hurt you. I never meant to."

"Oh, Frank!" She took a deep breath and got up from the sofa. She ran her hand through her hair and paced. A thousand threads of complexity tightly intertwined themselves into a restless ball in her stomach.

He got up, walked over to her, and pulled her into a hug. He kissed her forehead, and she rested her head against his chest.

"I have to tell you something," she said, backing out of their embrace. "I should be honest with you too."

He looked at her curiously and motioned to the couch for them to sit back down. "Tell me what?" His nervousness returned.

She was slow to respond. "There's something about me you should know too."

"There is?"

"I um…I know how you feel."

"What?"

"Your feelings about being gay, Frank, I understand them."

Losing Control

He thought back to what Terrence had suggested about Brianna. "What are you telling me?"

"I'm saying that I'm lesbian—"

"He was right..." Frank acknowledged aloud, cutting Brianna off.

"Who?" She inquired.

Frank looked at Brianna curiously.

"Hello? Are you going to answer me?"

"Huh?"

"Who was right? What are you talking about?" She was anxious.

"Terrence," he admitted.

"Terrence?"

"Yeah. He made a comment—said that he had thought my relationship with you was a cover for both of us."

She was surprised. Neither of them spoke for a moment, mulling over the flux of truths that were beginning to fill the room.

"He wasn't speaking negatively," Frank finally continued, "it was more of an observation that he'd held privately."

"Mm."

"So it's true then? You are."

"It is." She locked eyes with him in a moment void of humor. "My virginity was taken by a woman. I knew I was attracted to women before I knew what a lesbian was."

Frank listened quietly.

"You're the only man I have been with in almost a decade and one of two in my entire life."

"A decade? What—I mean, how?" He stopped to gather his thoughts. "If you're a lesbian and I'm bi or gay or whatever, what do you call what you and I had?"

"Call it convenience."

He pondered her statement.

"We could call it fear or a false portrayal of heterosexuality although I wasn't purposely sleeping with you to look heterosexual. I was lonely. You've been my friend, and I love you too. It just…I don't know."

Frank moved closer to her. "I wasn't using you as a cover either. At least not consciously. Actually, I'm not sure. I'm sorry."

"Don't be sorry, be yourself."

"I don't know who that is. I thought I did until recently. And us, what are we?" Discomfort infiltrated his words.

"We're friends." She smiled at him. "Frank, I guess there are a lot of things that we could call what you and I had, but after it's all said and done, I believe it was a convenient relationship for both of us. There's love between us, but it's not the type of fulfilling love that a straight couple has."

"Yeah."

Brianna touched his hand. "It's okay. Everything is okay. Take your time to get to know who you are. You don't have to box yourself in so quickly, or at all." She laughed. "Listen to me. I need to take my own advice."

"Oh boy," Frank chuckled. "Well, tell me more about this side of you. I feel like I'm getting to know you all over again."

"You never questioned my sexuality?"

"Not until Terrence brought it up. I just thought you were absorbed with your career and yourself. You know how you can be."

"Frank!" She feigned hurt feelings.

"What? Come on, you have to admit that you can have tunnel vision. Brianna. Brianna. Brianna. It's all about you."

"Hmph! Yes, I guess I can admit that. I don't want to, but it's true. I'm going to work on that." She actually did feel stung by his revealed perception of her. She didn't like coming off so selfish.

"Come here." Frank pulled her into an embrace. "Thank you for being a friend," he whispered. "Why don't we start again?"

She eased out of their hug and looked at him with a smile. "I'd like that."

The tables had turned and Brianna began sharing her feelings. She left out details about Pam, only telling him about her past relationships and experiences. Their conversation was long and they had only scratched the surface. They wanted to talk more, but fatigue got the best of them. It was late in the night when they went to bed. Frank spent the night in Brianna's bed for the first time in a while, but they were not intimate. They fell asleep in an embrace that was familiar yet had a new feeling to it. They wanted to remain friends although Frank was still saddled with the hidden truth of Yesenia. He only hoped that it would never come up again. He really wanted to keep Brianna in his life.

Brianna didn't want to lose his friendship either. She thought she could get over his act of betrayal in time and hoped that they would grow stronger now that they had a better foundation. She valued him and had many fond memories with him from their school days to the present that she would hate to abandon him in anger or jealousy. They had both made mistakes.

Chapter 15

"Morning, Anderson," Sheldon said as he walked into the headquarters, wearing a navy blue suit with a white dress shirt.

"Hey!" Brianna smiled. She was running on caffeine and had gotten an early start on the day. "I see we have a staff meeting planned for this morning."

"We do and I have information that you'll be happy to hear." He placed his briefcase down, took off his jacket and sipped his coffee.

"Oh, really?"

He smiled. "Yes."

"What is it?"

"Well, if you would have answered your phone or had the decency to call me back last night, you would already know."

"I'm sorry. I didn't see that you had called until this morning."

"I'm not even going to ask what you were doing."

"Good because it's none of your business," she teased. She also didn't want to become distracted by thinking about everything that happened the previous evening.

"It's my business if it's getting in the way of your winning this election."

"Oh, Sheldon, stop it. Would you just tell me what the good news is?"

He rolled his eyes. "Yeah. Anyway, you are in very good shape. You're not hurting for campaign dollars and a friend of mine at the Rockville Gazette tipped me that they're going to publish a feature on you this Sunday. A poll they just ran shows you having 58 percent of the popular vote in the district, and 18 percent of those respondents said that this was their first time voting!"

"Morning." Yesenia walked in, interrupting their conversation.

"Good morning," Brianna said.

"Hey there," Sheldon added.

"How are you guys?" Yesenia glanced at Sheldon and then looked Brianna in the eyes. She spoke without energy, almost as if she were forcing cordiality. Something was missing. Though Brianna was able to carry on as if the events of the night before weren't weighing her down Yesenia was not. She wondered how Brianna hid her feelings so well. She and Frank had to have talked about his gayness after the restaurant incident. Didn't that revelation shake Brianna up?

"It's time for our staff meeting, ladies," Sheldon said. "Come on."

The three of them walked into the main room of Brianna's headquarters where they met for a half an hour with the other members of her team. Sheldon went over all of the statistics and checked the status of everyone's duties. He rallied them and urged them to try to get more of their friends involved in the campaign.

"We have just a few weeks left to get Anderson's name in front of as many people as possible," he said and paused.

"I know all of you have worked very hard and I really appreciate your volunteering," Brianna added. "We just have to push through the final stretch of the race so we can have the much-deserved victory party!"

The staffers nodded in agreement as she and Sheldon took turns speaking. When the meeting was over, everyone dispersed to complete their tasks. Later that morning, the local news station called just as Brianna had returned from trekking across her district to meet with people. The producers wanted to run a short story on the sewage problem in part of District Five and reached out to her for an interview. It was just the kind of opportunity she needed!

"This is great," Sheldon told her. "As a matter of fact, let me see if Asad can drum up some of his friends to meet you there. I'm sure the reporter will have some people looking pissed off in the background, but I would rather she ask a fan of yours for his reaction than someone who might squander the opportunity to validate you."

"I thought Asad was helping Yesenia with the mass mailing that has to go out tomorrow."

"He is. Don't worry, I'll stuff the envelopes and let him go. He has a way of coming up with help on short notice. The media knows I'm your manager and won't ask my opinion of you. Asad or one of his friends will have a better shot."

"All right, thanks," she concurred.

Sheldon winked at her and smiled. Brianna still had a bit to learn about strategy, but he was still proud of her. If she could stay focused, she would go far. Brianna soon left for the interview and Sheldon took over for Asad.

Brianna's confidence soured when she arrived at the interview to find that Smith was already there. She was stunned. The news station made no mention of interviewing them both, and she wondered what was going on. Thanks to a tip from Yesenia, Smith was able to beat Brianna there. She made it appear as if she were already in the neighborhood to hear the plight of the residents. Though Brianna did get some camera time, she was angered that Smith got more and wondered how she knew to be there. Smith didn't give a damn about those residents.

Pamela and Eric talked as the muted television flashed images of Brianna on the evening news.

"I'm not sure what else to say or suggest," Eric confessed. They had talked at length about their fight and their feelings. "What am I supposed to do?" He crossed his arms against his chest and looked at Pam.

"I don't know."

She didn't want to go to a marriage counselor because she felt that there was nothing one could tell her that she didn't already know. She had two choices: stay or leave. Her feelings were always going to be there and *nothing* would make them go away.

"Pam?" Eric looked at her in disbelief. "You don't know?"

She began to cry. She knew that he was agonizing. The pain was in his eyes, his voice, and his body language. He was hurt and angry.

"Tell me, Pam," he raised his voice, "how am I just supposed to stop loving you?"

Her tears fell faster. "I'm sorry, Eric. I don't know."

"You want to leave. I'm telling you again that I don't want you to go, but I can't force you to stay."

"I didn't say that I wanted to leave."

"But you can't stay if you want to be with a woman instead of me." He exhaled. "So what do we do now?"

The more Eric asked Pam to make a decision, the more she thought about seeing a marriage counselor. If nothing else, the therapy might help Eric realize they should separate so that she wouldn't have to muster the strength to say it.

"I need a drink," Eric said and went in the kitchen. Frustration was building inside him like a typhoon. He knew he shouldn't turn to alcohol, but he didn't know how else to quell his feelings. He couldn't even hug Pam without thinking that he might no longer have her in his arms. Reality seared him.

"Maybe we *should* go to counseling," she finally said.

Eric turned around quickly.

"I want to at least try." She felt guilty for making him feel the way he did. "Let's at least try before we do anything else."

Eric put his empty glass down on the counter and walked back over to her. "All right. Let's do that." He was hopeful.

"I'll look for one and make an appointment."

"Okay."

After that inch of progress, Eric wanted to be alone, and Pam didn't object. It was uncomfortable for them to be around each other with the thick cloud of uncertainty hanging over their heads.

While Eric retreated to their home office, Pam began making dinner. Fearful questions filled her mind as she moved about the kitchen. Was she making the right decision? It would not be easy to start a new life. Was she ready to be single again? Though she wasn't fulfilled with Eric, he was familiar. He loved her and would do anything to protect her. Eric would break his back working to get her whatever she wanted. Was she ready to climb out of her safety net in order to find Ms. Right? What if she couldn't find Ms. Right and spent the rest of her life chasing a fantasy and missing what she'd had? Was it worth the risk?

Pam was standing on the edge of her comfort zone wondering if she would crash in loneliness and regret once she jumped or if she would fall into the loving arms of a woman. Her interaction with Brianna was not a guarantee that anything stable or long-term would become of them, and it just seemed too easy for it to be true. If she left Eric, it wouldn't be for Brianna, but for herself. As she diced onions, cut peppers, and prepared their supper, she tried to keep herself together but found it difficult. Pam wanted to curl up and cry, yet she was tired of crying.

Upstairs, Eric sat quietly behind their big oak desk. He leaned back in the office chair toying with a pair of stress relief balls as his mind traveled back to when he had met Pam. He was just getting grounded in his career path as a civilian at the time. Eric had served four years in the Navy and upon his discharge continued his education and obtained a masters degree in mathematics. The first company he worked for was the one at which he was still employed. He'd started as an associate and gradually advanced to being a credentialed Fellow of the Society of Actuaries and senior consultant at the firm, earning over $175,000 a year base salary.

The night he met Pam was one of chance. A colleague of his had an extra ticket to a New Year's Eve gala and convinced Eric to go to the party just two days before. Pam was one of the first people Eric saw when he arrived. While he was waiting to pull into a parking garage, she was one of two women he noticed getting out of a black, chauffeured Lincoln town car just a few feet away. Pam caught his eye immediately. Tall and regal looking, she stood out among the crowd waiting to enter the building. She had on a beautiful ruby evening gown that accented her every curve. Her hair was short back then, bringing attention to her beautiful dark brown skin. Despite the chilly night air, Pam stood with grace and captivated his attention. Eric watched her as she and her friend walked into the building and was suddenly glad he'd gone through the aggravation of going to four stores to find a tuxedo that fit.

Losing Control

Eric checked his tie, his collar, and his personalized cuff links. He ran his hands over his wavy low-cut hair and winked at himself in the mirror after he'd finally parked. He knew he looked good and was confident in his ability to engage the beautiful woman he had seen in the ruby dress. And he did. He and his colleague and she and her friend shared a friendly conversation as they ate. Before they had too many drinks, Eric offered Pam his card and she accepted. She also gave him one of hers.

Two days later he sent her a bouquet of Stargazer lilies and pink roses with purple larkspur in a crystal vase. His note simply read, *Happy New Year –Eric*. It was on fine stationery and delivered at the start of her day. She called him immediately and they began dating. Eric smiled at the memory. Things seemed to happen so effortlessly with her. They had few arguments and worked out their major differences over the first year of seeing each other. It was as if they were meant to be. Eric's smile faded into sadness as the smell of dinner brought him back to reality.

When she had told him early on that she was attracted to women, she had also said that she wanted to live a normal life. He had told her that he didn't believe in homosexuality and thought that she could live a normal life if she just met the right man. He was certain that he could be that right man and gave it his best shot. Now he realized that his best shot wasn't enough. Eric had to admit to himself what he'd done and it hurt. He had married a lesbian who he hoped he could make straight. There was no other man who could love Pam more or better than he could.

Eric could hardly stand all of the feelings that were brewing inside of him. His head and heart were aching. What was he going to do if she wanted a divorce? Eric was old-fashioned and believed that when he took those vows, he took them forever. He did not have a plan B and had no interest in another woman. He sighed, hoping that they could work things out. Tears crept into his hazel eyes but he brushed them away. He lowered his face in his hands and prayed that his marriage would not end.

Pam, too, was in turmoil as memories flooded her mind. She recalled how badly she had wanted to believe that the right man would make her straight, but deep down she knew that was untrue.

She and Eric dated anyway, their love growing with time although she never felt complete. Pam honestly wanted to be heterosexual and tried her best to bury her yearning for women. They were unwelcome and complicating her life. She tried praying them away and even saw a psychotherapist in secret for a brief period. He told her not to be ashamed of what she felt and that it was natural. He warned her that it would be difficult if not impossible to suppress her desires forever. She tried anyway and eventually settled into a routine with Eric. It was easier than dealing with the truth.

"Eric!" she called. "Dinner's almost ready!"

"I'll be right down." He got up lethargically.

Now things were hard. They had a home, a time share, two cars, and a motorcycle. They had investment portfolios, insurance policies, and more than one joint bank account. Pam didn't want to think about how complicated and heart-wrenching a divorce would be. She put the thought out of her mind for the time being and tried to have a normal evening with Eric.

Chapter 16

"I think we should slow down," Frank said to Terrence.

Terrence was upset with himself for the scene he had caused outside Christo's. Frank told him that he had to come out to Brianna as a result, even though he wasn't ready to.

"Frank, I'm really sorry about that, man."

"Don't worry about it. What's done is done and I can't do anything to change it. I just think you and I would be better as just friends."

"Yeah…I know…" Terrence understood why Frank was pulling back, but it still hurt to be rejected.

"You're a great guy, T. You're my best friend—a wonderful man, but I'm still trying to find my way. It wouldn't be fair to get involved with you as more than a friend right now. We're at different stages in our love lives and I'm not able to give you what you need."

"It's cool. I understand. You like those Latino boys anyway," Terrence joked, trying to lighten the mood a little bit.

Frank laughed. "Are we all right then?"

"Yeah, we're good, man."

"Cool."

There was a moment of silence as they both thought about their situation. They were at Terrence's house and he soon turned on the television to break the silence. They flipped through the channels and finally settled on the evening news. Frank knew the current discomfort between them would eventually fade. He was certain that he and Terrence didn't need to be in a romantic relationship. Frank believed some friends should remain friends because romance could ruin their bond. It might take a little while and Frank might even have to distance himself in the process, but he and Terrence *could* go back to the way they used to be.

"So how did things go?" Brianna asked Pam. They met for dinner at a small Italian bistro just across the Ben Franklin bridge in Philadelphia. Eric was out of town on business.

"As best they could, I guess," Pam responded. "I don't know. I mean, I know what's got to happen. I just don't know how it will all unfold." Pam told Brianna the details of her talk with Eric and her suggestion to try marriage counseling. She admitted that she didn't believe the sessions would save their union, but agreed to go in part to soothe Eric as well as to let him come to the realization that it was over. She felt like a coward after sharing.

Brianna took a sip of her water and spoke. "What do you want, Pam? Do you want to stay or do you want out?"

Pam placed her fork down and looked at Brianna. "I want to be happy. I want to feel like I'm living my life for me. I want to feel complete."

Brianna didn't respond.

"But I'm afraid of the transition."

"Is that fear going to stop you?"

"No," Pam answered softly. "I have to do it. I've reached a point where the burden of staying is outweighing the comfort of it."

Brianna sighed. She wiped her mouth with the linen napkin and looked at Pam. "I'm sorry. I know it's hard. I wish I could do more than just listen. I can see that it's taking a toll on you."

"Is it that obvious?" Pam chuckled, unsure of what else to do to not become sadder. In the back of her mind she knew that she shouldn't even be around Brianna. The temptation to reach across the table and touch her hand was great. Pam should have been avoiding her but wasn't strong enough to do what she knew was right. Her feelings were knotted up inside of her with her mind and heart pulling and tugging at it.

"Yeah, at least to me it is," Brianna answered.

"Would you like me to take these?" the waitress interrupted them. She motioned to their empty plates.

"Yes, please," Pam answered.

"All right," the waitress continued.

"I think we're ready for the check," Brianna said.

"Sure. I'll bring that right over."

"Thanks," Pam added.

There were only a handful of other patrons in the restaurant. Pam wondered if Eric was calling their home phone while she was out. It was still relatively early in the evening, and she could tell him that she was working late if he questioned her whereabouts. Normally she would never have to think of alibis or excuses. Normally she didn't worry if he would call to check on her, but nothing was normal anymore.

"When is Eric coming back?" Brianna asked. Her question yanked Pam out of her thoughts.

"Not until this weekend. He's in Ohio now and he has a stop in Indiana for a day before he comes back."

Brianna wanted to see Pam again while Eric was away. She felt culpable for her longing but couldn't help herself. The passing weeks had intensified her yearning for Pam, despite the potential danger in the situation. She wanted to taste Pam, to inhale the scent of her skin, and to feel the warmth and wetness of her body pressed against her own in the throws of passion.

The waitress returned with a smile and the bill. "Here you go."

"Thanks," Brianna said, immediately taking the check. "It's on me this time," she told Pam.

Pam smiled. "Thank you." She felt incredibly fragile and wanted comfort.

When they left the restaurant, Pam asked Brianna to sit in her car with her for a little while to talk.

"Please? Just for a few minutes." She gazed at Brianna.

"Okay."

Pam really didn't have to ask her twice. Brianna's heartbeat sped up as she walked to the passenger side of Pam's shiny black Infiniti M35 and got in. Inside, Pam leaned back in the plush driver's seat and looked at Brianna. She reached over slowly and touched Bri's hand. Her eyes were brimming with desire. Brianna leaned closer to her, taking Pam's soft hand into hers. The car was silent.

Their breathing was deep and the intensity between them escalated rapidly. Pam felt a warmth between her legs. She closed her eyes and submerged into the tantalizing depths of the moment. Brianna glanced outside the car windows, trying to be cautious of her environment. She felt uneasy, paranoid even. She hated to break the moment, but her conscience wouldn't let her do what she wanted to do with Pam in a public parking lot.

"Pam?"

"Yeah?"

"What do you think of um…"

"What?"

"I was just wondering if you might want to come over to my place…for privacy."

"Brianna, I don't know if I'm ready."

"You don't have to spend the night. I just want a little more time with you, but I feel vulnerable sitting here."

Pam blushed. She hadn't thought about going home with Brianna after dinner. "All right. Just for a little while."

Brianna was delighted. "Follow me."

"I will."

Brianna collected her purse and got out of the car. She fought the urge to kiss Pam passionately before exiting. *Be patient*, she reminded herself.

It took less than 15 minutes for them to arrive at Brianna's condo. Once inside, Brianna took Pam's hand and led her to the couch. "Do you want anything?"

"No," she grinned nervously, "I'm fine."

Brianna was out of words. She moved in and kissed Pam tenderly. Pam moaned when she felt Brianna's lips against hers. Her entire body became hot and her center became wet. She slid her tongue in Brianna's mouth and their kiss transformed from sensual to aggressive and lust-filled. They both moaned in pleasure as the temperature in the room rose. Brianna ran her hand up Pam's leg, up her side and grazed her breast as all of the needing and wanting that had been building inside of her for weeks began to ascend to the surface.

Losing Control

Breathe, Pam reminded herself. Her arousal from their kiss was strong and evident as she too began to let her hands wander about Brianna's body. She cupped the back of Brianna's neck and let her fingers roam through Brianna's silky hair. Brianna lowered her hand down Pam's stomach to her thighs. Pam shivered and parted her legs in response. They slowed down and Brianna gazed at Pam as she slowly slid her hands beneath Pam's skirt. She made her way to the warmth of Pam's inner thighs and traced the outline of her womanhood before touching Pam entirely. She could feel the fluid of Pam's sex through her lace panties.

Pam breathed open-mouthed and heavily. "Mmm," was all she could muster as Brianna carefully slid her panties aside and touched her. She tightened her legs, closing Brianna in while adjusting to feel more of her touch. The strength of Pam's adulterous moment with Brianna was hypnotizing. On his best night of foreplay, Eric couldn't compete with making her feel the way Brianna just did with a simple graze of her fingertips and a kiss. When Pam finally reached a climax it would be colossal. The heat between her legs burned like scintillating embers against an ebony sky, gradually rising like an orange moon claiming the night. Feverish flurries of excitement traveled throughout her body as it begged for more. She wanted to feel Brianna's fingers slide inside and feel her warmth, become slick from her wetness and be gripped by her walls. Pam wanted to venture down the path that would lead her to ecstasy but they didn't go that far.

The sound of Brianna's ringing home phone annoyingly shook them out of their kissing and groping. They exchanged no words as they backed away from each other. Brianna licked her lips, ignoring the phone. She was eager to do more and looked at Pam slowly from head to toe, taking in every inch of her beautiful body. Brianna bit her bottom lip in restrained desire.

"Pam…" Brianna said softly. There was a pulse between Brianna's legs that was beating like a bass drum. She wanted to have sex and she wanted to do it *now*. Her body was dominating her mind. She could feel her nipples becoming erect beneath her blouse and her head becoming filled with a wave of thoughts that carried her into vivid fantasies of pure erotic bliss. The surge of images and anticipated indulgences sent a stream to the core of her womanhood. "Umm…" She searched for the right words to say. "I know I said I wasn't asking you to spend the night, but do you," she hesitated, "do you want to?"

"Yes. I mean, no. I'm not sure," Pam stumbled.

Damn it. Brianna knew she would have to deal with this but didn't want to. Not now! She felt like throwing a temper tantrum if they didn't just get to the point. Her body and carnal desires wouldn't loosen their grip on her.

"Pam. I want you and I know that you want me too." She sighed. "I realize this is difficult for you. It's very awkward for me too." It was as if Pam were dangling bait in front of her just to pull it back.

"We've already crossed the line anyway." Pam excused their behavior. A pang of guilt slammed inside of her. *What about Eric? What about our vows?*

"Yes, we have."

Pam's cell phone rang, jolting her. *Eric. What if it were him?* she wondered as she sifted through her purse to find the phone. She became flush with fear.

There goes the evening, Brianna thought. She was disappointed before Pam even picked up the phone. The pulse between her legs fizzled. When she saw Pam's face after looking at the caller ID, Brianna knew it was Eric. She could see the panic plastered in Pam's eyes.

Pam felt a lump in her throat as she debated answering. Brianna looked away rather than at Pam as she deliberated. Brianna felt like a foolish child as her fantasy began to disintegrate into reality. Pam didn't answer the phone. She didn't know what to say and would deal with Eric later. She touched Brianna's knee and looked at her apologetically for the interruption.

Don't do this. Brianna's mind began getting the upper hand over her body. *You'll regret it.*

"So…" Pam spoke. She was saddled by thoughts of her husband and the consequences of her pending infidelity. Though she and Eric might be on shaky ground, she knew she'd be compromising her honesty and integrity if she consummated her relationship with Brianna and that, *that* would nag at her more.

"So," Brianna said. "I guess we ought to call it a night." Their evening was over and she knew it. Pam needed leave so Brianna could get her head together. She could hear Sheldon's voice of reason, caution, and reprehension: *I haven't been busting my ass for you to go and mess it up now!* She was becoming entirely too distracted by Pam and needed to focus on winning the election and avoiding scandalous drama.

"Brianna?" Pam's voice was soft and timid. "I'm sorry."

Married people. Brianna suppressed the urge to roll her eyes. In the polluted remnants of their moment of passion, Brianna began feeling selfish. "It's not your fault," she said and adjusted her clothes and inched back.

"Are you upset with me?" Pam quizzed.

"No. Of course not," she said, not fully meaning it.

"I don't mean to lead you on, Bri."

"I understand your situation. It's okay."

Pam felt bad. She felt conflicted. "I should be going. Can I call you when I get home?"

Say no. "Yes," Brianna answered. *Idiot.*

Pam gave her a thin smile and got up. They kept their goodbye brief. "I'll call you," Pam assured.

"Okay."

Brianna sat silently after Pam left. She was disappointed. She was frustrated and she was lonely. She got up to make a cup of tea in an effort to relax. Just as she was about to turn on the television for a distraction, her cell phone rang. She thought it might be Pam, but it was actually Frank. He called seeking comfort. He was struggling in his own funnel of twisted emotions and hoped talking to Brianna would make him feel better. They were both stressed but managed to joke that things were simpler when they lived a lie.

She eventually hinted to him that she was interested in someone but that their situation was hampered with complexities.

"What do you mean?" Frank probed for information.

"She's married," Brianna answered flatly.

"Oh."

The phone line was quiet.

"Yeah," Brianna continued, sipping her tea. "She's unhappy and is on the verge of a divorce, but it's complicated."

Frank was taken aback by her candidness. He was surprised she would flirt with adultery considering her bid to be a public official but kept his thoughts to himself. He was sure that she knew the danger, and he didn't want to bring it up and make her feel worse.

The lights were on in the master bedroom and living room when Pam arrived at home. Her eyes widened and her upper body froze with fear. Her stomach felt bottomless. She opened her mouth in shock as her heart began to palpitate and bang against her stiff, flame-embroiled chest. Eric was home, she realized, since she hadn't left any lights on when she had headed for work that morning. *Oh God!* She swallowed hard, wanting to back out of the driveway, but she stayed still, in panic. No sooner had she completed the thought when the garage door began to open by Eric.

She watched intently as it slowly moved up and revealed his car and motorcycle. He was standing next to the door that led from the garage to the house waiting for her. She parked her car and sat nervously before finally going in. Eric was still dressed for work although his tie was loosened around his neck and his sleeves were rolled up to his elbows. He glared at her in angry silence. His face was sour. Pam tried to coach herself to act as if she were just working long hours, but found it too difficult. She knew Eric wouldn't buy it.

"Eric? What are you doing home?" she asked.

"Where were you?"

"I was um…" She hadn't the words to appease him.

"Pam." His voice was deep, stern, and questioning. He was not in the mood for lies. "I went by your office and you weren't there. I waited there for an hour in case you had just stepped out, but you didn't come back. You didn't answer your phone when I called you either."

She put her purse and briefcase down but didn't say anything.

"So," he cleared his throat and continued. "Where were you?"

She didn't respond.

Eric stretched his fingers and balled them into fists. He released them and placed his hands behind his neck in restraint as he waited for Pam to explain herself.

"I thought you were in Ohio," she finally said, trying to deflect the focus back to him.

"My meetings got canceled, Pam, okay? Now answer my question!"

"I was out. I went out to dinner," she confessed.

"Dinner? With who?"

She didn't answer him immediately. Instead she looked around the house and noticed open mail scattered on the coffee table next to his laptop, which was also open. She could see from where she was that one of the papers on the table was from the phone company and wondered if Eric had been searching for proof that there was someone else. Eric never went through the mail.

"A friend," she said.

"Her?"

"Who?"

"*Her!* God damn it, Pam, don't play me for stupid. You know who I'm talking about!"

"Calm down."

He looked at her like she was crazy. "Calm down?" Eric was getting angrier.

"It was just dinner," Pam lied.

"You went on a *date*?" He wrapped his mind around the truth. "Is that what you did when you thought I was away on business?"

"Eric—"

"I don't believe this shit! You're *still* a married woman!"

"Eric, please!"

"Please what?" He pounded his fist against the wall. "Shit, Pam! What happened to trying? What happened to counseling? I guess you were just *waiting* for me to leave so you could go out with your girlfriend!" Disgust laced his words.

"She's not my girlfriend!"

"Well, whatever the fuck she is then! She's *obviously* someone! There *is* someone else in your life!" Eric walked toward her.

Pam had a flashback to their last argument and tried not to let her fear show. He had better not put his hands on her again. "Eric, please, all right? I messed up! I had no right to go out to dinner with her." She took a step back.

He clenched his teeth as he listened to her. It was taking all of his strength to contain his anger and pain.

"I'm sorry." Pam couldn't think of anything else to say. She really didn't want to beg for his forgiveness. She didn't want to deal with him at all.

"That's it? That's all you have to say for yourself? You're sorry?"

"What do you want me to say!"

"I want you to say you're not going to see her anymore! I want you to say that you meant it when you said we'd try to work it out! God damn it, I want you to say that I'm not losing my wife to a woman!" His voice was rough yet vulnerable.

Pam saw the stress lines forming on his forehead, the redness in his eyes, and the perspiration on his pink dress shirt. "I can't," she said softly. "I'm sorry, Eric. I can't."

"Yes, you can! Say it. Tell me this is just a rough patch that we can get through," he pleaded.

"I wanted to mean it when I suggested counseling. I really did, but deep down I didn't think it would help. I can't change my feelings. I am who I am and can't deny or ignore it anymore."

Eric became worn out with the topic. His anger morphed into something unreadable. He reached for her and held her arms at their sides. "Pam, please. You didn't even give counseling a shot." His eyes were full of despair.

She sighed. "I don't think it'll help. I should have said that in the first place."

"So this is it?"

"I don't know."

"Are you saying we're over?"

"I don't know! I need space! I need time! Eric, I just…Please!" She walked away from him. "I need space," she repeated.

He rubbed his chin, looked upward, and then back at her. "You want to separate."

"Yes," Pam answered without hesitation. It was time.

Out of words, Eric just glared at her and then walked away. He grabbed his jacket and motorcycle helmet and left without acknowledging her decision. He needed space too. He needed to cool off.

It was almost 2:30 in the morning when Brianna's ringing phone woke her out of a deep slumber. The high-pitched sound startled her. Bleary-eyed and barely awake, she glanced at the clock before getting up to search for the phone.

"Hello?"

The caller hung up just after she answered.

Brianna rubbed her eyes and pushed the light that displayed the caller ID. It was Pam. She had never called that late before. Although Brianna had waited for her call earlier, she was unsure how to respond about getting it so late. She crawled into bed and debated calling Pam back. *Don't do it.* She had to deliver a speech the next morning and needed her rest. Brianna plugged the phone back into its charger and decided to ignore the call.

Five minutes later she picked it up again and pressed redial from the caller ID but got no answer. She hung up before the voice mail completed the number announcement. It seemed odd that Pam wouldn't pick up the phone after calling her, but she let it be. It took Brianna almost an hour to go back to sleep. When her alarm went off at six o'clock she hit snooze four times and slept for another hour. A phone call from Sheldon finally got her out of bed. He was surprised that she wasn't up yet.

"Usually you would have already read the morning papers by now, Anderson," he said.

"I know. I'm just off to a slow start today. I'm up now."

"Get off your ass and get dressed. I want to go over your speech with you for some last-minute changes."

"Okay, I'll be there soon."

"Hurry up." he insisted.

"All right, Shel."

Brianna hung up and took a hot shower. She tried to wash away the baggage she brought on herself by getting involved with Pam. Over the last month and a half they had gone from tip-toeing around their sexuality to being drenched in desire for one another. As the steam built up in the shower, she closed her eyes and tried to relax. Thoughts of Pam trampled through her mind, but she needed to clear them and zone in on her career. Brianna was exhausted from the race and eager to get to Election Day. It was only two weeks away but wasn't coming fast enough. She quickly finished grooming and left for her headquarters.

While Brianna rushed to get to work, Pam sat in her office with suffocating panic. She sat alone behind closed doors, unable to concentrate on any task. She asked her administrative assistant to deflect all interruptions unless it was an emergency. Pam didn't even know why she went to work. It would have been less nerve-wracking had she stayed home. She sighed and decided to call Brianna.

"Hello?" Brianna answered on the second ring.

"Hey," Pam responded, her voice shaking.

"Pam, what's going on? I tried to call you back last night but you didn't answer."

"What are you talking about?"

"Last night. By the time I'd gotten to the phone you'd hung up. When I called back I didn't get an answer."

What is she talking about? Pam's heart sank into a cavity of fear. The free fall into worry momentarily interrupted her ability to speak.

"Hello?" The silence on the line made Brianna nervous.

"Brianna, I didn't call you last night."

"What?" She almost slammed on the brakes.

"I didn't call you," Pam repeated.

"It was your name."

"Shit…" She checked her cell phone to look for record of a missed call. It was there. She hadn't noticed.

"Wh—what do you mean, *shit?*"

"Shit!" Pam exclaimed. "Eric was home when I got there."

Brianna pulled over immediately. "He was what?" Her eyes widened and her stomach lurched as if plummeting to the bottom of the ocean. Her body went cold, yet she was perspiring.

"He wasn't in Ohio. He was at home," Pam fretted.

"I thought you said he was traveling on business." Brianna thought her body was going to cave in on itself and crumble. She could feel sweat building on her back and her body warming up.

"He was supposed to be," Pam responded, "but he said his meetings had gotten canceled."

"Oh, Jesus." Brianna closed her eyes and shuddered. The poison of Pam's nectar was beginning to manifest itself. She had barely tasted it. She could feel the hairs on her arms rising in terror. *Stay calm*, she told herself. "What happened?"

"We had another argument and I finally told him I need space. I told him that I think we should separate."

"What did he say?"

"Nothing. He left." As the words left her lips, Pam logged into her e-mail account to see if Eric had left any trace of having been in it. She had checked it the evening before when he left the house but didn't notice anything unusual. She was aware that he could have read her messages and then marked them as unread, but didn't think much of it since there weren't any messages from Brianna. They did not send e-mails or text messages. "Hold on for a second, Bri."

"Yeah…"

Pam didn't have any old phone records in her e-mail account either.

"My caller ID had your name on it." Brianna couldn't wait anymore.

"Are you sure it had my name and number?"

"I don't know about the number. I was asleep, but I'm certain it said Pamela Thompson. He must have gotten your phone."

Pam closed her e-mail and logged into her mobile phone account. She and Eric were on a family plan with their cell phone provider and she was the account holder. Her name would show up on a land line Caller ID whether it was her or Eric calling.

"How did he know what number was mine? Did you delete your phone records? How did he know!" Brianna spoke without stopping to breathe. She was horrified.

"Yes, I deleted everything connected to you."

Pam had not been careful enough. Although she did take some precautions, she had not counted on Eric becoming obsessive about finding out who the other woman was. She didn't think about him hiring a private investigator to trail her. She hadn't anticipated that he'd install a keystroke logger on their home computer two days before she had changed her passwords. She hadn't been quick enough. Eric had recorded every single thing she'd typed, including her old and new passwords. He had screenshots that were taken every 30 seconds while Pam was online.

While Pam was at work writhing in misery, Eric was in a hotel room stewing over photos of her and Brianna at dinner, in Pam's car and walking into Brianna's condo, all compliments of his private investigator. After his argument with Pam, he had called his investigator and asked for any evidence of infidelity. He did not want to wait until the investigator got something solid. He wanted anything that would get him closer to at least knowing who the woman in Pam's life was, and he wanted it immediately. Now he had his answer. He hadn't gone home because he didn't think he would be able to control his temper if he saw Pam. His agony was too fresh. It was too raw. He needed time.

"What do you think he's going to do?" Brianna questioned Pam.

"I don't know."

"Oh, fuck!" Brianna swore. "God damn it!"

"Shit, I'm sorry!" Pam paused. "Shit, shit, SHIT!" She pounded her fist against her desk.

"Just um…don't worry, okay?" Pam ran her hand over her head and gripped a handful of her own hair. She tapped her hand nervously, let go of her hair and banged her desk repeatedly with her fist.

"Don't worry? What? How the hell can we not worry, Pam?" The pitch of Brianna's voice grew higher as she spoke. She was having an anxiety attack.

Sheldon soon called on Brianna's other line, and she knew she had to hang up with Pam. She was running late, and he reminded her that they needed to go over changes to a speech she was to deliver that day.

"I have to go, Pam. I'll call you back as soon as I can."

"All right."

Brianna rushed to her headquarters. Sheldon pulled her into an empty room as soon as she arrived and plainly asked her what was going on. She dodged his questions, but he made it clear that he knew that it had to be *someone* affecting her.

"Anderson, I've already told you to stay focused. You've been fortunate thus far to have a clean race and to be more popular than Smith, but don't take it for granted. She'll eat you for breakfast if she identifies a weakness. Whoever it is that has you distracted needs to be put on the back burner until after the race is over." He spoke firmly. "Can't you just wait?"

Losing Control

Brianna wasn't in the mood for his lecture but could do nothing to stop him. He went on incessantly and was aggravated with her the whole time. They were fed up with each other by the time he stopped scolding. Brianna was more fed up and disappointed in herself. She wanted to take a day off but couldn't. She had to function at full capacity in the middle of her drama and not let it show to the public.

"Let me see the changes you made to my speech," she said, trying to get back to work. She glanced at the clock and noted that she had to leave within the hour.

"Here." He handed it to her.

Brianna was grateful that Sheldon only had minor changes, as she had already memorized most of it and didn't want to rely on her notes when she gave it. It was hard enough to push thoughts of Pam and Eric out of her mind without having to worry about fumbling over a speech.

Chapter 17

Terrence was already at the auditorium when Brianna arrived. Frank and Terrence had helped organize the event in conjunction with other Rutgers-Camden alumni, current members of their fraternity, and its sorority organization. The room quickly began to fill with students, members of the community, and a few reporters who looked like they'd rather be somewhere else.

"Good morning," Brianna said after being introduced. She cleared her throat and glanced at her audience. Her eyes passed over the attendees without stopping at any one person. Her black skirt suit with a lavender blouse was chosen to exude energy, but her classic black pumps were already beginning to make her feet ache.

"Thank you for such a generous and warm introduction," she continued and smiled at the moderator. "I'm very happy to have been invited here with you today. Your support means a tremendous amount to me. You, the people, have revealed that you care about Rockville. You care about repairing and revitalizing the 5th District. You care about your home. You care," she paused, "as much as I do, about *our* home."

She moved away from the podium and began to walk back and forth across the stage as she spoke. She needed to move to help her stay focused on where she was and what she was there to do. She noticed Terrence slip out the back of the room while Frank remained. Did he leave to tend to his barbershop or did something happen between him and Frank? She even noticed Yesenia in the third row sending text messages or playing a game on her cell phone. Either way, she wasn't paying attention. Brianna's mind was all over the place.

Brianna returned to the podium to look at her notes. "In the last decade, Rockville has gone from the ninth poorest city in the United States to the fifth. More than forty-five percent of the city's families live in poverty," she said. "We have people on the streets, living in filthy ghettos, run-down project buildings infested with roaches and rodents. We have too many honest, working poor people who have to rely on non-profit organizations to help them put food on the table every month; too many kids who don't have clean parks to play in." Her words seeped into the minds of her listeners.

"You have the power to change the direction of this city starting with District Five. Each and every one of you sitting in the audience has that power. In the last election, the participation rate was only 31 percent. That means that all of you who didn't raise your hands earlier when I asked who voted are the key factor. You have the power to put the right people in office…"

Brianna used a cocktail of charisma, eloquence, and intellect to urge her audience to be active in the upcoming election. A decent round of applause rose from the room when she finished speaking. She was grateful that the distractions of her love life didn't cause her to make any mistakes. Afterwards, she participated in a brief Q & A session before preparing to leave. A number of people wanted to shake her hand before they left. The last one was Eric. He walked up to her without a smile. Without a word. Unbeknownst to her, he wasn't the slightest bit seduced by her oratory, nor was he a fan.

"Hello," he said stoically.

She could tell immediately from his stance and dark, heavy presence that something wasn't right. "Hello." She spoke with a smile despite her instant discomfort.

Only Sheldon, Frank and Yesenia and a few others were still lingering. Frank and Yesenia had managed to behave professionally despite their break-up. Brianna, however, now felt uneasy.

"Do you know who I am?" Eric asked. His eyes were locked on hers in an angry gaze.

"I'm afraid I don't," she answered. *Eric.* She couldn't recall any description of him from Pam, but her gut told her that this must be him.

"Really?" he quizzed.

"Should I?"

Eric's stare dug into her. He remained silent to let her answer her own question. He could sense Brianna's apprehension. Irritation churned inside of him as he stood face-to-face with the woman who, in his mind, was stealing the affections of his wife.

"I'm afraid I don't know who you are," Brianna repeated.

"I need to talk to you in private."

"I beg your pardon?"

"You need to come into the hallway and talk to me unless you want me to cause a scene."

Brianna clenched her teeth. She looked back at him with steely eyes of fearlessness. It was manufactured, but she didn't want to appear weak and show any more uneasiness than she may have already revealed. "Fine," she said and began walking out, leaving the members of her team in the auditorium without notice.

Yesenia was watching though. Seconds later she exited the room too, but there was no way that she could eavesdrop without being noticed. Curiosity swirled inside her as she walked back inside.

"I know what's going on between you and Pam." Eric got right to the point once he and Brianna were alone.

"Excuse me?" She responded with the same curtness with which he spoke to her.

"Don't act like you don't know what I'm talking about."

"I don't." If Brianna had learned anything from her political experience thus far it was that in the face of extreme pressure and fear she *had* to hide her feelings. And if necessary, lie.

"Pamela Thompson. I know that you two have something going on."

"I don't know what you're talking about."

"I wonder what Colleen Smith would do with this information if she knew it."

Brianna swallowed hard. Just then Sheldon, Frank, and Yesenia came out of the auditorium and into the hallway.

Frank looked Eric up and down, wondering who he was and what was going on. "Everything okay?" he asked, noticing Brianna's uneasiness.

"Everything is fine," Brianna answered.

"Are you sure?"

"Yes."

"Okay." Frank looked at Eric once more. He didn't want to leave her alone with him.

"Just give me a minute and I'll be outside, guys" she said.

"All right," Frank said, as he left the building with Sheldon and Yesenia.

Frank wanted to know who that man was. So did Sheldon. Sheldon wanted to know if he, Eric, was the person who was distracting Brianna. Yesenia was trying to think of a reason for her to stay behind but had none. She passed the time by trying to figure out who that man might be and why Brianna needed to be alone with him. Why was there tension between them?

Eric pulled out a photo of Brianna and Pam at the restaurant. "Do you know what I'm talking about now?"

"What do you want from me?"

"Do you know who I am!" Annoyed, Eric spoke louder.

"I already said that I don't." She raised her voice to match his.

"Yes, you do. And I know you do. I'm Eric, Pam's husband." He pointed at Pam in the picture. "Have you slept with my wife?"

"What? No!" *Shit!*, she thought. *How the hell did he get that photo?* Brianna was alarmed and outraged. If she weren't running for office she would have crushed Eric's manhood with a stronger arrogance and self-confidence than he had. She would have told him how desperate he appeared in approaching her the way he did, but she couldn't. Eric clearly had the upper hand, and she had to tread very carefully over these troubled waters or she might drown in scandal.

"So explain this."

"It was a business dinner," she lied.

"Business dinner my ass. I know she went home with you." He showed her the other pictures he had. "I'm telling you right now you better stay away from my wife." As he looked at Brianna, taking in all of her feminine features, he suddenly felt inferior as a lover, yet powerful as a man.

Brianna labored not to show her nervousness. Sweat was streaming down her back.

There was a moment of thick silence before Eric spoke again. "Look, if you don't want this to get out, I suggest you to stay away from Pam or I *will* leak this."

Brianna's jaws tightened. Every muscle in her body tensed. She wanted to tell him to go fuck himself, to stop acting like a bitch, to swat him like a fly. The need to stifle her natural response left a bitter taste in her mouth. She cursed herself for getting into this situation. She felt tormented trying to figure out how to get through it unscathed. "I think we're done here," she said and turned to leave.

"With one phone call," Eric followed her, "I can crush your image. All of this talk about honesty and caring and values that you're seducing people with would be nullified by the truth that you're a fucking home wrecker!"

She stopped and responded quietly but sternly. "I did not break up your marriage. It was already damaged before I even met Pam." *Fuck.* Brianna let her emotions get ahead of her and spoke when she should have remained silent.

The truth stung Eric, but he scored. He was taping their conversation, and though it wasn't a blatant confession of adultery it was something to go with his pictures.

"Besides, she and I are just friends. There is nothing to tell."

"If I can't have Pam, then neither can you. I will ruin you both." Eric wanted to make everyone involved hurt as much as he did, even if he might be embarrassed in the process. "Just try me."

"You don't mean that," Brianna said calmly. She smiled.

He was surprised that she was calling his bluff. "Yes, I do."

Frank re-entered the building to check on her. "Brianna?" he called from a few feet away.

"Just a minute, Frank."

Frank stood still. He stared at the two of them.

"Is that your boyfriend? Does he know you're a dyke," Eric taunted. His behavior seemed childlike to Brianna.

"Excuse me, but that is none of your business. I have to go," she said, walking away.

"Stay away from her!" Eric hissed as she left him standing alone and walked toward Frank. "Cunt," he mumbled as he watched her leave.

As Brianna made her way to the exit, she wondered if she'd handled Eric properly. She plastered a smile on her face to mask her anxiety, but Frank saw right through it.

"What was that about?" he asked immediately.

"I'll tell you later. Is everyone still out there?"

"No, they left. Sheldon said he and needed to work on another engagement for you. He wants you to call him as soon as you can," Frank said. "Tell me *now*. Who was that guy and what was that about?" he questioned as they walked outside.

Brianna was embarrassed to tell Frank the truth. The longer she stalled the more he began to concoct his own answer, which was the truth.

"Was that her husband?" he asked as they got into the car.

Brianna was silent. Discomfort, fear and anger barricaded her response.

"Did he threaten you?"

"Frank!"

"What? Answer me then! I didn't like anything about the way he looked. It's obvious you're uncomfortable, and I know something is wrong, so just say it! Because if he does *anything* to you I'll—"

"Yes, okay. That was him and yes, he threatened to tell Smith everything if I didn't stop seeing his wife. He said he'll ruin both of our careers." She omitted the pictures, afraid to say too much and embarrassed to admit her carelessness.

Frank was angry. "Both your careers? Who is his wife? And are you going to stop seeing her?"

"Yes, but I don't know if that'll really stop him. He doesn't realize that Pam's going to leave him regardless of me or anyone else. He has already lost her. Shit, he never really had her." She paused. "Fuck!"

"What?"

"Sheldon is going to be pissed."

"Of course he is. Who is this guy's wife?" Frank asked again.

"Pamela Thompson. The city treasurer."

"Oh, shit…"

Brianna ignored Frank's response. "I have to tell Sheldon because I need advice on damage control just in case." She pounded the steering wheel. "Fuck! I knew better than this. I knew *better* than this!" she repeated, scolding herself.

Frank ran his hands over his head.

"I need to talk to Pam. I need to talk to her to see if she can calm him down."

"Leave that woman alone, Brianna."

"I'm going to. I just—"

"Leave her *alone*," he reiterated. "You *have* to."

Brianna groaned. "I know."

Brianna finally caught up with Sheldon at her headquarters. "I need to talk to you," she said.

"Fine, we need to have a sit-down anyway."

"Alone," she added. "Yesenia, thank you so much for your help today. You can go now if you want to."

"Okay. I'll see you guys tomorrow then." Yesenia got up and slowly walked over to where her purse was. She wanted badly to stay and hear what Brianna would divulge, but didn't get the chance. Damn it.

Brianna waited until Yesenia was out of earshot to begin telling Sheldon about her dilemma with Pam and Eric. As she anticipated, he was livid.

"Oh my fucking, God! Anderson, why? Why!" He could hardly contain his disappointment with her as she told him everything that was going on.

"*Did you* sleep with her?"

"No!"

"Good. Did you kiss her?"

Brianna didn't answer him.

Her silence was taken as a yes. Sheldon sighed. "Where? I hope not in public. I hope he doesn't have a picture of *that!*"

"No. The photos he had were just of us in a restaurant and in her car." She paused. "And in front of my condo."

Sheldon exhaled loudly.

"We didn't kiss in public. We did in my condo, but that's it. Please just help me be prepared if he does say something," she pleaded.

"Of course I'll help you fix this mess. You just better hope it's not too late. I'm disappointed in you."

"I know. I'm sorry."

They couldn't talk much longer because Brianna had more appointments before the day was over.

"If this comes out," Sheldon advised before she left. "I mean, if he has more evidence than you think you're going to have to own up to it." He paused to think. "You would have to get Pam to agree to that of course, but that's what I feel you should do. Don't deny it, because if he has any way of proving his allegations you'll look dishonest and despicable. You'll be done."

Brianna listened to him quietly. Her nerves were rattled the entire time he spoke. *How am I supposed to get Pam to agree when I'm not supposed to talk to her or see her?* She tried to think of a way to make that happen, but was at a loss.

"You'll want people to see that you're strong enough to not be ashamed of who you are. Strong enough to be held accountable for your mistakes." His words were actually comforting.

She nodded in agreement. "Are *you* okay?"

"About what?" he asked, not looking at her.

"With me…how I am—*who* I am?" She spoke softly, timidly.

Sheldon looked up at Brianna with soft eyes. He was a little surprised at her question. He cared more about the effects of her actions on her campaign than about the core of her dilemma. Her question brought out his tenderness. "Of course," he said. "Anderson, that's your personal business. I don't look at you any differently or see you as any less than I did before. I just wish you would have used better judgment." He touched her shoulder. "I'm old. There isn't much that I haven't come in contact with already. I don't care."

She smiled. "Thanks."

"As a matter of fact," Sheldon said, getting back to business, "you need to start working on a statement tonight just in case."

"All right." Brianna looked at her watch. "I have to go," she said. Brianna felt a little better. She felt lighter, freer, having told him.

"I will." She grabbed her purse to leave. Once inside her car, she dialed Pam.

"You have to do something about Eric," Brianna said as soon as Pam answered the phone.

"Hang on," Pam responded. She got up to close her office door and returned to the phone. "All right, I'm back. What are you talking about?"

"I just met your husband."

"What!"

"He came to the college where I spoke this morning and threatened to go to Smith if I didn't leave you alone."

Pam's intercom beeped. "Hold on, Brianna." Perturbed, she unwillingly accepted the incoming call.

"Excuse me, Pam?"

"Yes, Yolanda?" she responded to her administrative assistant.

"I have the mayor on the line for you."

Shit. Pam's gut sank. Without knowing the reason for the call, she immediately thought the worst. "All right, give me a second to clear my other line and then send her through. Thanks." Her heartbeat galloped in fear, filling her mind with a dust-like haze.

"Brianna?" Pam said when she returned to her line. "I have to take this, it's the mayor. I'll get back to you as soon as possible."

"All right." *The mayor? Eric wouldn't! Would he?* Eric didn't say anything about going to the mayor about this! Brianna felt asphyxiated by the grip of fear.

Pam's mood brightened when she began conversing with the mayor and found out that an order was coming to her to look into Smith's spending accounts. A full breakdown of Smith's reimbursements for the last three years was being requested, as well as immediate research into which non-profit organizations received money from Smith's discretionary funds.

"The Department of Investigation is conducting a probe into her, Wiley and Ferguson," the mayor said, citing two other standing members of council. She spoke matter-of-factly.

An internal examination was being launched into how all three of them were spending city funds, as accusations had been made by the Chief Administrative Officer that over $800,000 had been funneled into non-profit organizations, some of which weren't even real and others at which council members had relatives on the board.

"I'll get on it now," Pam responded as they hung up.

If Smith had allegations of fraud hanging over her head, Pam surmised, then it would certainly detract from any drama that might come out about Pam and Brianna. Pam wanted to call Brianna back but decided to get started on Smith and take care of business first.

    She was eager to begin digging into this scandal. Hundreds of pages of paperwork would have to be pulled from files and analyzed. It was unusual timing to begin such a probe just a week shy of Election Day but a fortunate twist of fate for her. It was the leverage that Pam and Brianna needed.

Chapter 18

"You can't say anything about this to anyone," Pam told Brianna after sharing the news of Smith's investigation. "It's confidential and I could get in a lot of trouble for even telling you."

"I won't. But what about Eric?" Brianna asked as she glanced at the evening skyline from her bedroom window.

"I'll deal with him when I leave here."

"Do you think you'll be able to keep him quiet?"

"I should be able to. Don't worry. I will," Pam said as she retrieved electronic financial records. She wasn't really confident that she could influence Eric, but she hoped so. "I do have to hang up now, but I'll call you later tonight if I can. If not, then in the morning."

"All right," Brianna said. She hung up and tossed her cordless phone aside before stretching out on her bed. She was extremely exhausted and had a nagging feeling of loneliness. All of her fears and anxieties were sucking the life out of her, pulling her strength. She glanced at her laptop sitting next to her and sighed. She couldn't seem to concentrate hard enough to begin writing the statement that Sheldon told her to.

When Pam finally got home, she could tell that Eric had been drinking. She could smell the liquor on him. She could see it in his eyes as well as his sloppy posture as he stared at their entertainment center. Pam stood in front of the television and looked at him. He peered back through eyes that barely met hers.

"Eric?" she called to get his attention.

"Hm?" he grunted, still not looking directly at her.

She thought about the best way to speak to him. She didn't want to come right out and ask about his visit to Brianna, but she didn't want to drag it out either. "What did you do today?" she inquired.

"I went to work," he answered flatly. He leaned back on the couch, his head against the back cushion and eyes closed. He exhaled.

Pam sat down in a chaise diagonally across from him. "You did?"

"Mm hmm," he mumbled, finally bringing his eyes to meet hers. "I did."

"Eric," Pam paused.

"What, Pam? What?"

"Did you really go to work today?"

"That's what I said, isn't it?"

"It is, but I think you were elsewhere."

"Oh really?" He sat up straight.

"Eric, did you go see Brianna today?" she finally asked. She tried to be cautious and control her tone.

"What?"

"Did you?"

He looked at her with a disappointed smirk on his face and shook his head in disgust. He sucked his teeth and then got up, walking away from her and into the kitchen. It hurt him to even have her question him as if she were so concerned about Brianna. Fuck Brianna. What about him? Pam's question dug into his heart like a shovel forcefully breaking the earth and gutting it of soil.

"Answer me, Eric."

"Why? If you're asking, then you must already know. You wouldn't even assume something like that out of the blue, so it must mean that she told you after I specifically told her not to contact you!"

Pam felt assaulted by his snap. "Why would you do that, Eric?"

"I can't believe you have the nerve to ask me that."

"How dare you go and threaten her. Who do you think you are?"

"Who do I think I am? I'm your fucking husband, that's who I am!" he yelled loudly. "Who do you think *you* are?" Eric's eyebrows furrowed in boiling anger. Pam's audacity pissed him off. "What do you think *you're* doing? Are you even thinking at all? Or are you too fascinated with your fucking dyke fantasies to realize what you're doing to us?" He reached in his pocket and threw the pictures at her. "You think I don't know!"

His words hit her like a two-punch combo and the sight of the images almost crippled her. Wounded and put in her place, she changed her approach. "Why didn't you talk to me instead of going to see her?" She regretted the question the moment it fell from her lips. Tears began to form in her eyes. "Eric, I know what this looks like."

"It looks like you finally got what you wanted!" he slurred.

She moved closer to him. "Honey, no—"

"Don't 'honey' me! Don't fucking patronize me! Just from you coming to me the way you did lets me know that she probably called you the moment I left!" His eyes were ablaze with anger. "I warned her."

"What about *me*, Eric?" Pam was hurt. "I told you that nothing happened between us and we're just friends."

"And you expect me to believe that bullshit? You have a lot of nerve."

"It's true!" she yelled.

"You're lying! The proof is right here!" He pointed at the photos.

"That only proves we went to dinner. I already admitted that!"

"You didn't say shit about going to her place afterwards so stop fucking lying to me! There is something there. I could see it in Anderson's reaction to me that something happened between you two."

"No, Eric." She looked at him with eyes brimming with tears and fear. "I don't know what you thought you saw, but it wasn't that. It wasn't a confirmation of anything. I'm telling you that nothing happened between us. Please," she said and reached for him. "Please…"

Eric snatched his arm away from her. He wanted to believe her, but tussled with doing so.

"I thought you loved me," she continued. "Would you really do what you said knowing that it would ruin my career? Eric, *nothing* happened between us. I've been faithful to you." Every word that fell from her lips tasted of sour hypocrisy and selfishness, but she had to say what she could in hopes of swaying him. She was ashamed of herself. "Listen to me," she said softly. She ran her hands down his forearms and then took his in hers. "I'm so sorry for causing you pain. Despite my own struggles, I do love you. Just hear me out."

Her touch made his heart shatter. "I don't believe you. I can't. I mean, I love you too. I always have—even now when I want to hate you, I can't. All of this shit I've done; I did it to try and keep you, but I just don't know." He paused. "I don't know if I can forgive you or forget what you've been doing."

"I haven't *done* anything. Don't you believe me? She's just a friend."

Eric glared at her. "You're looking me in eyes and still lying to me!" he yelled. "Pam, listen to yourself; oh my God! I don't even know who you are anymore! If she's just a friend, then why did you go on a date with her?" He was seething. "Why did you go *home* with her?"

"What? Eric, calm down, please."

"I will not calm down! I can't." Pain swallowed him as he looked at her. "This is all bullshit. It's just one lie after another with you," he said. "Even if you didn't sleep with her, your heart is with her."

"It's not!"

"It isn't with me!" His voice cracked. "I get it now. We're over. There's nothing I can do…" He began putting on his jacket.

"Wait!" She grabbed him by the arm and touched his face, running her fingers across his cheek. She looked into his hazel eyes with a soft, apologetic stare dampened by her weeping. "Eric…" Pam didn't want him to leave. Her body was rigid with panic, and it was killing her to see him fall apart.

Eric felt the years of his marriage jamming his throat. Her caress brought him to the edge of tears, but he knew not to be won over by her touch. She was a liar and a cheat. This wasn't the woman he married. "Let go of me, Pam." He pulled his arm away, sweat forming at his brow and temples. "It's clear that we're over. I don't even know why I bothered," he said as he put his shoes on. "*Now* you want to get worried. *Now* you want to act like you still love me. No, fuck that. Fuck this. Fuck it all. You chose that bitch over me…fuck you!" he said bitterly and walked out. Jealousy and anger spread like wildfire from the center of his heart throughout his body, intensifying with each passing moment.

Pam was speechless. She couldn't find anymore words to beg him. There was no use. She watched him put on his helmet, get on his bike, and ride away without another word to her. In that moment, she knew that their relationship had been severed, and it was her fault. She'd handled everything all wrong. Not only had she broken his heart, she'd grinded it to bits.

Deep down, Pam hoped that his love for her would ultimately keep him from exposing her and Brianna to Smith. It was that hope that prompted Pam to call Brianna and tell her not to worry. Brianna couldn't help but worry. The surge of deeply suppressed desires had drowned her with poor judgment, and she could hardly breathe, much less lay in the pain-soaked bed she'd made.

Chapter 19

"I'm giving you this information in hopes that you'll know what to do with it," Eric said and then stood up. "I don't want anything in return, just break her down." It had been along day for him. He had traveled to North Carolina and back on business and then went straight from the airport to see Smith. He had told her all of his thoughts and played the secret recording that he'd made of his talk with Brianna.

"You do realize that leaking this won't hurt just Anderson and your wife, right?" Smith asked. She was delighted that Eric swooped in with the slanderous information that she needed to put a smear on Brianna's clean image. At the same time, the fact that Brianna's affair was with the city treasurer made it tricky to handle.

"I don't care anymore," Eric responded. "It is what it is." He looked at her once more and nodded acknowledgement of her warning before walking out of her small office.

She would have to collaborate carefully with her manager, Tony on how to use the information. If Pam knew that Smith was behind leaking it, then Pam, as city treasurer, could make it difficult for Smith to access funds if she remained councilwoman. And there was no guarantee that Brianna would lose the election over this hearsay, not even with Eric's tape. Brianna didn't admit to anything, despite Eric's accusation of adultery. The photographs didn't prove anything either.

On his way out of Smith's headquarters, Eric brushed past Yesenia. He apologized for bumping into her and although he didn't recognize her, she placed him from the auditorium. She immediately wanted to know what he was doing at Smith's base. He had the same aura of anger about him that he did the previous day. She excitedly made her way into Smith's office without wasting another second, but Smith held up a finger to instruct Yesenia to give her a minute before interrupting. She was on the phone with Tony.

Outside, the skies had darkened with storm clouds. The temperature had dipped into the 40s and rain began to fall through the chilly autumn air. Eric flipped the collar up on his jacket and walked quickly to his car with his head down. He was numb. The pain that he had felt had gone flat. He thought about requesting a leave of absence from work, but it would be difficult to do so. He realized now that he didn't mean it when he said he didn't care about the consequences of airing his dirty laundry. He would be embarrassed in front of his colleagues and local clients when news of Pam's affair became public knowledge. He would look like the victim, but that position was still unflattering. All of the emotional fuel that drove his miscalculated actions had dissipated and he was now empty. He had no more steam. He was tired and starting to feel regret. Pam worked hard to get to where she was. She was brilliant and had been handpicked for the position. It was going to be a hard blow when she got exposed, but she hurt him first.

Yesenia tapped her hand against her leg impatiently as she waited for Smith to wrap up her telephone conversation. She began trying to put the pieces of the puzzle together.

"Well, a day late and dollar short; I don't have anything to offer you," Smith said to her, interrupting Yesenia's internal quest for the truth.

"What? Why?"

"I'm afraid you didn't bring me good enough information in time. Do you have any idea what I just found out? Anderson is a lesbian and she's having an affair with Pamela Thompson!" Smith spoke louder than she intended to. She was still giddy about the gossip.

Yesenia was annoyed. *She* wanted to be the one to hand Smith information that got rid of Brianna. She wanted that career boost Smith promised her in exchange for bringing Brianna down.

Smith shuffled papers on her desk and said, "You had all the time in the world to find out some dirt, and you didn't even know what was going on in your own camp!"

"I'm just a volunteer coordinator. There was only so much access I had!"

Smith shrugged.

"Wait, what if I could give you information to humiliate Anderson even more?" Yesenia asked.

"What are you talking about?"

Yesenia thought about Frank. "There's more to her than you know."

"Like what?"

"Would we still have a deal if you win the election?"

"That depends on what you know."

Yesenia paused before speaking. She then spewed gossip of her own about Brianna based on her limited knowledge. "Frank, the guy she was dating is gay too. It was all a cover."

Smith didn't know how the information would help. "So? She isn't married to him, is she? And weren't you sleeping with him too?" Smith's face contorted in confusion.

"Can't you use that to make her look worse? And yes, I was with him, but I didn't know he was a faggot at the time. I'm sure now." *Ugh.* She thought of being with Frank now knowing the truth about him. As she spoke, Yesenia regretted the moment she became locked in a parasitic embrace with Smith. She didn't like the needy feeling she experienced when speaking to her and the constant feeling of being bled of control over her own destiny. "I'm sure you can spin it into something to further taint her image. 'A web of lies or something?'"

"Maybe," Smith responded. She toyed around with a ballpoint pen.

Tony walked in wide–eyed, with a smirk on his face. "Eventful day?" He nodded and acknowledged Yesenia.

"Like you wouldn't believe!" Smith answered. She had already told him over the phone about the information she'd received from Eric.

The three of them remained behind closed doors. Yesenia made her case again in front of Tony, and Smith finally said that she'd think about using the information regarding Frank. Smith then made it clear that she needed Yesenia to step out. She had work to do and meetings to attend, but more importantly she wanted to talk to Tony alone. Although she was certain she'd win the race, a small part of her recognized that it would not be wise to have Yesenia know too much about what she was doing in case Brianna *did* win.

Chapter 20

Eric didn't go home that night. He couldn't go to that house. He didn't want to see Pam or anything that would remind him of her. He'd still had his laptop and work documents from his trip to North Carolina and decided to check into a hotel. He thought it would be better to get some work done to take his mind off Pam but found it extremely difficult to shift his mind to his job. Trying to keep up with his work while being bogged down with his personal issues had taken a toll on him. In an effort to relax, he ordered dinner with a bottle of red wine from room service. It hardly worked. An hour later Eric still couldn't focus on his calculations or settle his mind enough to comprehend a phonebook-size document on regulatory changes to pension plans.

"Shit!" He threw his pen against the cherry wood desk. Putting his face in his hands, he rubbed his temples, trying to ignore the painful throbbing in his head. As Eric sat in the silence of the hotel room, he became somber. Quietly, he cried. He had been restraining his tears since the beginning of the downward spiral of his marriage but saw no point in stopping them now. He was alone. As the warm drops slid from his eyes and rolled down his cheeks, he closed his eyes tightly as if to shield himself from the pain he felt. As he wept, his torment seemed to ease slightly and just temporarily, but it was at least a short-lived reprieve from his illness: heartbreak.

Eric wasn't accustomed to crying and could hardly remember the last time he had allowed his tears to be released. They stung, as if were mixed with bleach.

Pam called Eric repeatedly but finally gave up. She realized that he was in a hotel by logging into their bank account and checking the recent purchases. There was a hold from Marriott. It relieved and saddened her at the same time. She paced, unable to remain still in their big, empty house as rain poured down outside. It was cold and lonely. She'd called Brianna and they had talked until they were too tired to speak. Pam felt as though she were stuck inside a nightmare, tormented. Her conversation with Brianna was laced with fear and anxiety. They wanted the whole ordeal to be over.

Pam slept fitfully after hanging up with Brianna. The sheets on her side of the bed were damp with sweat and the empty space where Eric normally lay was cool and untouched. She woke up haggard and hurt but honest with herself. It was still raining outside as she began getting ready for the day. Today she vowed to do damage control. She had no choice.

Sheldon was at Brianna's condo before she was dressed to leave. He'd called with news that she did not want to hear. "We've got a *big* problem," he stated the instant she answered her phone. "I'm coming to see you." He spoke hurriedly and was there before Brianna knew it.

"What is it, Shel?" she asked as soon as she opened the door for him.

Sheldon's stare was piercing. "Smith knows about your affair."

"What?" she gulped, the bottom of her stomach falling out.

"I got an anonymous phone call this morning about you and Thompson."

"From who?"

He looked at her like she was stupid.

She *felt* stupid. "I mean—how do you know—"

"Whoever it was is trying to blackmail you out of the race," he cut her off.

Brianna thought about the information that Pam had given her regarding the investigation against Smith. Anger began to rise in her as she thought about being blackmailed and her promise to Pam not to reveal the damaging news she had about Smith. "No, fuck her. Fuck Smith! I am *not* dropping out of the race."

"I know you're not. Did you write the statement I told you to?"

"Yes." Brianna was furious.

"Let me see it," Sheldon said and rubbed his forehead.

Brianna got the printout and showed it to him. While Sheldon went over it line-by-line she called Pam. After three rings, Pam picked up.

"Smith knows," Brianna warned.

"How do you know?" Pam asked worriedly. The hairs on her arm stood up as if a chilled breeze had just passed over her.

"Because she's trying to blackmail me out of the race."

Sheldon looked away from Brianna's document and directly at her as she spoke into the phone.

"Don't worry, Brianna. I'll deal with her. I'll deal with her right now," Pam responded.

"What are you going to do?"

"I have to go."

"Wait, Pam. What are you going to do?"

"I'm just going to have a talk with her."

Brianna had an inkling that Pam was going to bring up the investigation, but she didn't want to say so in front of Sheldon. She exhaled. "Okay."

"I'll call you later." Pam hung up.

"What was that about?" Sheldon inquired.

"That was Pam."

"I gathered that," he replied sarcastically. "What did she say?"

Brianna was silent.

"Anderson, I can't help you out of this mess if you leave me in the dark. Tell me what she plans on doing."

"She said she's going to talk to Smith."

"And say what?"

"I'm not sure, but I'm guessing she's going to let Smith know that she can't blackmail me so easily. Smith's got her own closet full of skeletons that I'm sure she doesn't want displayed to public. The Department of Investigation is looking into her for allegations of fraud and misuse of public funds. She doesn't know it yet," Brianna said. "They're investigating her, Wiley, and Ferguson."

"Oh, yes." Sheldon smiled broadly, speaking in a delighted, deep voice. "That's just the kind of shady shit I want to hear! I'll be damned. It's about time!"

"Mm hmm," Brianna agreed. She smiled uneasily. She was still worried. "I don't know how Pam is going to handle this."

"Don't worry, any way she handles it will quiet Smith."

"How do you know?"

"Because if Smith persists and you bow out—"

"I'm not!"

"I know, I'm just saying. If she does, then Thompson can recommend and probably get permission to freeze Smith's discretionary funds going forward. Thompson has the power and clout to get Smith's ass out of office disgracefully. If Smith backs off now and lets the race run its course, then at least if she loses, she goes out with no embarrassment. She'd be a fool to push this one," he said.

Brianna mulled over his words and became more comfortable as she waited for a call back from Pam. In the meantime, she and Sheldon polished her just-in-case statement for the press should her affair with Pam become public.

Pam pulled into a parking space right next to Smith, and they met eye-to-eye before a word was said.

"Hello," Pam muttered, simmering inside.

"Hi. How are you?"

Pam nodded positively and forced a smile. "I'm well, and you?"

"Oh, you know. I'm holding up."

"Mm hmm." There was a dark, dry silence between them before Pam spoke again. "We need to talk," she declared.

Smith leaned against her car. "About what?"

"I don't have time for games, Colleen."

"I'm not sure what you're talking about, Pamela."

"We need to talk about whatever it is you think you're going to do with the information my husband gave you." Pam watched Smith's eyes to see if she would give any indication of guilt. She gave none.

"Excuse me?" Smith continued to play ignorant.

"Eric. I know that he spoke to you."

Smith looked at Pam blankly, refusing to diminish her perceived leverage.

Pam stepped closer to her and spoke in a loud whisper. "You should be very careful about trying to blackmail people. I know what you're up to and advise you not to push this any further."

Smith said nothing.

"If you think the only person who will get burned is Anderson if you force her to bow out of the race, you're sadly mistaken. Be careful not to start a fire you can't put out. You might get reduced to ashes." Pam's last statement was emboldened with bitter contempt.

"Are you threatening me, Pamela?"

"I'm warning you." She gained confidence with every word. She had power.

"I'm not sure why." Smith's eyes judgmentally took in Pam's presence. "I don't even know what you're talking about," she said, stubbornly denying knowledge of the blackmail attempt.

"I have three words for you: Department of Investigation."

Smith's eyes widened as Pam continued to speak.

"Think about that," Pam said. "You think about what you've done in the past, your questionable fund allocations to non-profits, and decide if your blackmail scheme is really the smartest thing to carry out against Anderson considering it involves *me*."

Smith clenched her teeth and listened to Pam's words. Her breathing got heavier. Anxiety rushed inside her as she stood in silence.

"Don't fuck with me, Colleen. I'll shatter your career and you'll go out limping and licking your wounds just like Iseman," Pam said, speaking of the former city treasurer whom she had replaced. He'd left his post in shame. "Drop it. Let the race run fairly and let the voters choose, unless you like the taste of your own blood." Pam surprised herself, even frightened herself by her threat. It felt as though someone else were speaking for her.

Smith moved away from Pam, looked her in the eyes, and then walked away.

Brianna called Frank as soon as she got a free moment. She was overwhelmed with the blackmail threat but she wasn't going to give in. She hadn't spoken to Pam again and didn't know what had transpired between Pam and Smith. Talking to Frank would comfort her.

"Three days left, are you ready?" he said after they exchanged hellos.

Brianna sighed.

"What's the matter?" He could sense something was wrong with her by her weighted silence.

"I really messed up," she began. She was interrupted by a clicking noise in the phone.

"Hold on a sec," Frank said. There was a brief period before he came back to her. "Never mind. That's just Terrence on my other line. I'll call him back. What happened now?"

Brianna went on to tell him all the gritty details of the blackmail attempt that had seemingly come from Smith. Frank's skin tingled as he listened to her. He couldn't help but think about himself as the words flowed from her lips. *What if someone exposed me?* he wondered.

"I should have been more careful," Brianna said, interrupting his fearful thoughts.

His silence indicated his agreement with her. She *should* have been more careful. Much more careful. It was too late for that now though, and he didn't want to make her feel any worse than she already did. Besides, he hadn't always used his best judgment either. "What are you going to do?" he asked.

"I'm waiting to hear back from Pam. She had some dirt on Smith and said that she would take care of this situation for me."

"She needs to take care of her husband too." There was a boom of annoyance in Frank's voice when he spoke of Eric. He wanted to exchange words with Eric in defense of Brianna, but he didn't want to become wrapped up in this drama. He wasn't ready to confront his sexuality head on the way Brianna was. Franklin liked his private life.

"I don't know what to say about him," Brianna responded. She was angry at Eric yet finally understood his actions. She had taken part in wounding him in one of the worst ways possible. Without intending to, she had stolen his wife. She had stolen his life.

Frank's line beeped again.

"Brianna, I have to take this call," Frank said.

"All right." She paused. "Frank?"

"Yeah?"

"Do you think you could come over for a while tonight?"

The tone of her question surprised him. It had a familiar softness to it, akin to when she *used to* request his company. It was vulnerable and Frank missed it. It made him feel needed. It made him feel normal.

"Yeah, I can come over."

Brianna felt strange. She noticed the difference in the way she asked her question too. She wanted comfort, but why did she want Frank's? Why not Pam's? Even if she did want Pam, she realized, she couldn't have her. Not right now. Not for a while, at *least*. And even that was a hope, not a certainty. She needed someone.

"Thanks," she said gratefully. "I'll see you later."

"Okay."

Brianna was exhausted as the day wound down. Even with Frank as a friend and Sheldon as a guide, she felt lonely and afraid. Brianna wanted to leave Rockville and go to a familiar place, temporarily at least, somewhere safe. For a few moments she dwelled on memories of the simple life she had before she decided to focus on her career, before she'd been seduced by the allure of power and leadership. Before she had grown up.

Brianna thought about her family. Her mother. Her grandmother. She missed them. *New York.* Oh, how she missed New York! She waded through mental images of her family, her friends, and her undergraduate experience at Pace University. Thoughts of the first and only woman that she'd fallen in love with floated across her mind like a gentle breeze over an endless body of calm, clear water. *Sadira.*

Brianna smiled at bittersweet memories with Sadira. Her fondest recollection was the chilly evening that Sadira had helped her pack her things for her internship. *Sincerity*. Sadira had given her the most thoughtful gifts. A grin spread across Brianna's face as she remembered the awe she'd felt after opening the packages containing two business suits—the right size—a leather-bound journal, and a gift certificate for a briefcase. *And the CD!* Sadira had written music for Brianna! The night was precious and full of tenderness. There were several other beautiful experiences with Sadira but only remnants of them were left. Brianna had purposely tried to forget the feeling of being entangled by a love that was long gone.

Reality choked her, interrupting her sweet reverie with acrid residuals. Back then she had been afraid of love—loving a woman—and now had an unquenchable thirst for the opportunity. Brianna's eyes glistened as she lay alone. She imagined several possible futures too. Images of Pam in Brianna's mind were so clear it was as if Pam had just appeared in the room. The vision was powered by pure desire. Craving. Brianna ached to get closer to Pam. She wanted to touch her, to spend many nights talking, laughing, and *loving* her. She couldn't help but wonder if she were being incredibly stupid for even entertaining such thoughts. What would happen with Pam and Eric? What would happen with the election? Would she win and live happily after Pam divorced Eric? *Yeah, right.* Again, reality crushed her fantasy before it even had the chance to crystallize. It was ruined.

Brianna sighed. She tried not to dwell too much on Pam. She didn't want to set herself up for heartbreak. *Too many what-ifs.* Things were just too fragile for anything good to come out of it, she told herself. Brianna's mind was noisy with unanswered questions. Could she climb to mayor, governor and possibly beyond without the support of a spouse? She didn't know. Brianna was finally extracted from her thoughts by the sound of a buzzer. Frank had arrived.

She got up to let him in. He was meticulously groomed as usual, looking as if he were a model who had just finished a photo shoot. His haircut was precise. His jeans were relaxed and without a wrinkle. His shoes were without a scuff, and his ashen sweater showed off his solid physique. She felt Frank's presence; his confidence enveloped the room even though he had just stepped in it. His scent was subtle and complimenting. His dark skin was smooth, accented by a beautiful smile that he flashed when he saw her.

"Hello, Councilwoman!" Frank exclaimed.

"Not yet, Frank." Brianna smiled, grateful for his immediate calming effect. Her dimples looked more pronounced than usual.

They greeted each other with a warm embrace.

"It will be." He brushed her hair away from her forehead and planted a quick kiss against her coco skin.

"Thanks. Come in and sit down."

"It's good to see you, Bri."

"You say it like it's been a long time since we've seen each other!" Brianna pushed him playfully.

"No, but the days feel so long, sometimes it seems like it."

"I hear that."

"So what's up?" he asked.

"What *isn't*?" She went to the kitchen to bring two drinks. "I'll be right back."

"All right." He turned the television on while waiting for her to return, flipping through channel after channel of what seemed like pure foolishness. He eventually settled on music programming, 90s music of all choices. Frank slid out of his shoes and set them neatly beside the couch. He leaned back, propped his feet up on the coffee table, and relaxed.

"Here you go," Brianna said when she came back. She handed him a cold beer and had a glass of wine for herself. The beer had been his anyway, sitting in her refrigerator since he'd bought it a month ago.

"Thanks." He looked at her with appreciative eyes.

She glanced at him again. How could she have not even suspected he was gay or bi? He was dressed way too well to be straight. She had been just too busy thinking about herself to question Frank's sexuality but now she inwardly laughed at herself for stereotyping him. He could have been just an old-fashioned pretty boy.

Brianna asked about Terrence. She was no longer jealous or hurt by Frank's fling with him.

"How are you two doing?" she wondered aloud.

"Fine. We're just friends."

Brianna looked at him suspiciously.

"Seriously."

"You two just reverted to being friends so easily?"

"There was discomfort at first but not too much. There was no need to make it complicated. We didn't really get far into a physical relationship, and deep down we both knew we should avoid it," Frank said. "Plus, I told myself not to nourish any more relationships that were built on convenience."

His words stung Brianna.

"That wasn't a shot at you or us," he said quickly. "I just meant that I learned from what you and I had. I'm still learning."

"Me too," she said softly.

"Yeah…" Their conversation stalled for a moment before Frank picked it back up. "So what's up with you and Pam?" he quizzed.

"I don't know," she confessed.

Brianna shared all that she felt for Pam. She wasn't sure if it was the alcohol or sheer loneliness making her divulge the desires of her heart to Frank. She held nothing back and soon realized that tears filled her eyes. She was so lonely. She wanted to call Pam but couldn't. All she had was Frank. Familiar Frank. She leaned against his chest, wishing it were Pam's.

"Don't worry Bri," he comforted. "Things will fall into place." He used his thumb to brush away a single tear that was threatening to slide down her cheek. A part of him wanted to kiss her while another didn't. He missed being needed and feeling like a source of strength for her. Frank was confused.

Brianna sat up and looked at him with hope shimmering in her eyes as if Frank had the power to assure her his words would hold true. He couldn't, but he hoped they would for her sake. He was barely out of the forest of loneliness himself.

"I better get going, Bri." He leaned forward and stretched.

"Thanks for coming over and keeping me company."

"Anytime." He smiled. "I'm always here for you." Frank turned the television off and put his shoes back on.

"Thanks." She walked him to the door and they hugged once more before he left.

The desolation in Brianna's heart returned the instant the door shut behind Frank. *Get it together*, she told herself. She lethargically cleared away the wine glass and beer bottle. Hands on hips, she let her eyes roam around her condo. Quiet. Her condo was too quiet. She turned on some music to help fill the empty air and drown the silence around her. *No love songs*. She changed the playlist several times before an instrumental wafted through the speakers. It was just what she needed to relax. No words, just music. *Relax*. She repeated the word to herself until it worked. She didn't even remember going to bed or falling asleep.

"You're going to have to let it play out fairly," Tony said to Smith. They were at her headquarters.

"I know. I can't stand that fucking Brianna. Shit!"

"Damn it, Colleen. You act like you can't win without the blackmail." Tony was starting to tire of dirty politics. A part of him actually wanted Brianna to win. The way he was accustomed to doing things was starting to suck the life out of him. Brianna was refreshing despite her personal life.

"I know I can. I should. I better," she huffed. "I just don't like her. She's shaken up too much. She's actually getting folks all riled up and thinking for themselves."

"She's young. She's hungry."

"Whose campaign are you working for!"

"Yours!" he lamented. "I'm just saying that you were the same when you started out. It only lasts so long before you realize that you can only do so much, especially on council's salary."

Smith sighed. "Whatever. We should have posted the pictures online anonymously instead of making a call." She regretted her strategy out loud. "I need a drink."

"Maybe, but don't worry. The race is still close. You can win, but you have to leave the tricks out of it." He got up and put on his jacket. "Come on, let's get out of here."

Smith rolled her eyes but followed him. She wasn't confident that she would win and it was eating away at her.

Chapter 21

"Congratulations, Anderson!" Sheldon exclaimed. "You did it."

Two days had gone by so fast she couldn't believe the race was finally over. Finally. Brianna and her team began celebrating before the polls officially closed. She *knew* she'd won.

"*We* did it, Shel," she said and beamed at everyone. "Thank you guys so much for all of your hard work. You have no idea how much I appreciate you!"

Yesenia forced a smile. Despite still being in Brianna's good graces, something about the whole experience still left her feeling less than victorious, and she was disgusted at the sight of Frank and Terrence. They made her tastebuds go sour. Yesenia was still kicking herself for sleeping with Frank. *Ugh.* She didn't feel as turned off by knowing Brianna was a lesbian, but that knowledge didn't make her comfortable either. All of it seemed so unnatural to her. She wanted to leave the party.

"Congrats!" Yesenia gave Brianna a hug. She had to admit that she had become a better actress over the course of the campaign.

"Thank you. I won't forget all of your hard work."

Stupid Brianna. Yesenia glowed. *That* made her feel better. Frank eyed the two of them from across the room and felt tension racing through his body. He swallowed hard, trying to cram his guilt down to the acidic center of his stomach.

In the midst of thanking everyone and accepting congratulations, Brianna felt her phone vibrate. The tremble of the device jolted her. She had been impatiently waiting to hear from Pam, and she hoped it was her. Trace amounts of perspiration built on her fingertips as she slipped away from the center of attention to check her phone.

Congratulations, Brianna. I wish I could be there with you right now.

It was a text message from Pam's new e-mail account. Brianna's body warmed with delight. She smiled at the message and began typing a reply.

Thank you. I wish you could be here too. She paused before sending her response, debating if she should tack on an indirect invitation. Was that too forward? Did it matter? Eric and Pam were over and so was the race. *It's too bad I can't see you tonight. I hate to have to spend it alone,* she added and sent the message. Her heart beat harder against her chest. Shit. Why couldn't she control herself when it came to Pam? For all of her book smarts, Brianna realized that some of her actions were downright moronic when it involved Pam. The race might be over but her career had just started! She brushed the feelings off. She was supposed to be happy. She managed a smile. *Be happy, damn it. You won!*

It was getting late and everyone would start leaving soon. Brianna didn't want to go home. Not to be by herself in her victory. She didn't want to be with Frank either. Not tonight. His company would feel patronizing, although she knew he would be hurt by her thinking that.

Her phone vibrated again. *I want to come see you tonight.*

Brianna froze. Had she read the message right? She read it again, staring at each word.

What's stopping you? Brianna typed in response.

"Are you heading home after this?" Frank asked, breaking her entrancement with her communications to Pam.

"Huh?" Brianna had barely heard him. She hadn't noticed him walk up.

"I said, are you going to go home when everyone leaves?"

"Oh," she paused. "Yes. Sorry."

Frank eyed the phone in her hand. She clutched it tightly.

"Is that her?" he questioned.

Brianna's eyes veered away from his. "Yes," she gulped.

"Be careful. Please, Bri. This is just the beginning for you."

She took his advice earnestly although frustration shrouded her. "I know, Frank." She slid her phone back in its holster on her hip and returned to the crowd.

Soon everyone started leaving. Sheldon, Frank and Brianna were the last to go. Brianna had assured Frank that she was fine and that she just wanted to relax at home. She was exhausted.

"All right," he'd conceded and walked to his car. "But call me if you need me."

"I will. Thanks."

"Goodnight.

"Night."

Brianna had only been on the road five minutes when her phone rang. She was just about to dial her mother before being cut off by the incoming call. She answered on the first ring.

Pam's voice was a song on the other end of the line, as soft and pure as a classical melody on a flute. It took her breath away. "Nothing is stopping me," she said, answering Brianna's last text message. It was a partial truth. She was afraid, and the weight of guilt was like a boulder on her shoulders. But Eric was gone.

"You really shouldn't tease me like that, Pam."

"I'm serious." Pam cleared her throat. "Eric went to visit his parents. He took an overnight bag."

"Are you sure?"

"Yes."

"So…"

"So, I um…"

Brianna slowed down and stopped at a red light. She tapped her fingers against the steering wheel. "So do you want to come over?"

"Yes, I do."

Brianna's stomach fluttered. She was delighted, driving quickly once the traffic signal changed to green. "I'm not at home yet, but I'll be there soon."

"Do you want me to give you time to relax?"

"No." Brianna answered too quickly. "I mean, you can come now if you want to."

"I do want to, but I'll wait a little while and—oh, I'll just come now." Who was she kidding? Pam didn't want to wait another second. She might lose her nerve if she did. She couldn't let that happen and then regret it later. The time was right. Eric had left just after the news had reported that Brianna had unprecedented support. He'd turned the television off and, with an attitude, began packing a bag. *I'll see you later,* he'd said. Pam heard his voice in her head. He had hardly glanced at her before walking out of the house. It was as if *he'd* just been defeated, and in a way, he had.

"All right. I'll see you soon," Brianna responded and hung up.

After Pam had gotten off the phone with Brianna, she went to the bathroom and stared at herself in the mirror. She wanted to smile but found it hard to do so. Her skin was hot with anticipation, yet she felt so burdened. She and Eric considered themselves separated, but they still shared a home. They were working on that. For the last couple of nights they had slept in separate bedrooms. Pam had left him in the master suite and taken to one of the guest rooms.

She looked into her eyes in the mirror. "How long have you waited for this?" she quizzed herself. *Too long.* Pam washed her face and brushed her teeth. She applied light make-up and strolled to her closet to change. *What should I wear?* She looked at shirt after shirt and skirt after skirt, not knowing what to choose. *What's the appropriate attire for infidelity?* She had to turn on a radio to distract herself. She was battling her conscience but refused to be defeated. She was being true to herself and had a right to not feel guilty about finally getting what she really wanted. At last, she decided on an evergreen dress with brown accents and earth toned jewelry to complement it. She dabbed tiny splashes of fragrant oil behind her ears and on her wrists. Her eyes passed over the inside of her palms as she applied lotion. She noticed the absence of her wedding band and engagement ring on her left hand, but she ignored the missing symbols of love and promise. She closed her fists and glanced at a mirror once more before leaving. *It's time to get out of this house.*

Brianna's heart leaped when she saw Pam in the hallway. She smiled broadly but contained the rest of her excitement until they were in her condo and out of view. The moment they were inside they embraced. Brianna inhaled the sweet scent of Pam's hair. It smelled like a mixture of pomegranate and mangos.

"Thank you for having me over," Pam whispered. "I know my situation made things difficult for you." She eased out of the hug and gazed at Brianna with sincere remorse.

"It's okay... Hey," she reached out, "let me take your coat."

Pam slid out of her brown outerwear and handed it to Brianna. "Thanks."

Brianna marveled at Pam's body, taking in her thin-heeled, knee-high boots, form-fitting dress, and rich, chocolate skin. Pam was a picture of elegance. "Get comfortable. Do you want anything to eat or drink? Want to listen to any particular music or watch television? Is the temperature okay?" She surprised herself with the cascade of options she poured out.

"Um. A drink will do."

"White or red?" Brianna asked, assuming Pam wanted wine.

"White is fine." She winked at her. "Are you always this hospitable to repeat visitors?"

"Of course."

"Oh, so I'm not special?" Pam feigned a pout.

"Sure you are," Brianna said, softly grazing Pam's face with her thumb. "I don't normally offer food and entertainment choices too!"

They both laughed, breaking the ice. Pam slapped Brianna's back playfully.

"I just want you to be comfortable," Brianna said. She took Pam's hand and led her to the sofa. Her fingers tingled when they met Pam's. She wanted her badly.

"How could I not be with you doting on me this way?" Pam meant it. She felt relaxed now. The air was light and fragrant and music was playing. It was faint, almost inaudible except for the metallic sounds of an instrument she didn't recognize. "Actually, it's me who should be pampering you on a night like tonight. Congratulations again."

Brianna broke into a smile. "Thank you. But you're in *my* house. I'll tend to you. So if there's anything that you need," she said, moving closer to Pam. "Or *want*." Closer. "Just let me know."

Pam felt the muscles in her thighs tighten. She could feel the ardent energy from Brianna's skin. If she had moved forward one more inch, their noses would have touched. The sexual power eclipsed the room's tranquility. They kissed. Pam leaned in first, her tongue expertly sliding against Brianna's. Brianna tasted of mints. Pam felt a minor pulse in between her legs graduate to a thunder. Her breathing picked up speed as she explored Brianna's body, kissed her cheeks, and tasted her neck. Years of wanting a woman were running out of her with intensity, clamoring for liberation. *Slow down.* She had to control herself. She had waited too long for this night to ruin it with haste. Brianna moaned. She didn't want Pam to slow down. The aggression was welcome. She wanted to be taken. And to take. Her body brimmed with heated desire.

Slowing their kiss to a stop, Pam ran her hands over Brianna's shoulders and down her arms. She caressed Brianna's body with curious touches.

"Where is your bedroom?" Pam finally asked, forgetting about her request for wine.

"Follow me." Brianna spoke quietly. She got up only to find her knees weak with anticipation. She clasped Pam's hand and led her to the master bedroom.

The fruity air was coming from the bedroom, Pam realized as soon as she entered. The scent was stronger in the room, and she noticed candles flickering. The music was louder too, not by much, but definitely a few decibels. The ambiance made her feel as if she'd stepped into a romantic chamber. She felt under a spell, wanting to strip out of her clothes immediately. She closed her eyes and inhaled, slowly. Exhale. She felt at ease.

"This is it," Brianna said, pulling Pam back to reality. She pushed up the dimmer for the room's lighting just a hair. She wanted to admire Pam's beauty without straining her eyes.

"It's nice." Pam's response was flimsy, but she didn't know what else to say.

The bedding was a mix of diamond blue and sandy brown, with decorative pillowcases. The room was neat, as if a housekeeper had just finished tending to it and the burning candles and enchanting sounds accented the suite perfectly.

"If you want to hear something else, I can change the music," Brianna offered.

"No, no. It's fine. It's very relaxing. Almost mesmerizing."

"Good. I'm glad you like it." Brianna smiled. "You're the reason I'm into it now. Well, sort of."

"Really?"

Brianna walked over to the bed and Pam followed. "Yes. Ever since the day at the spa with you, I've been hooked on this New Age, meditation music. It helps me wind down." She beckoned Pam to sit next to her.

"Well, I'm glad I helped you…sort of." Pam took the invitation to get closer to Brianna.

They shared a laugh and soon they were kissing again. The temperature began to rise. Both of them were becoming heated with passion. Brianna slid the straps of Pam's dress from her shoulders. She ran her hands against Pam's breasts, which were still partially covered by her clothing. Brianna's fingertips persuaded an erection from Pam's nipples within seconds. She could feel them hardening at her touch and longed to take them into her mouth.

Pam released a pleasurable sigh. She pulled Brianna's shirt off, exposing her unblemished, light brown skin. Brianna's breasts sat firmly in a silk lavender bra with lace trim. Pam's eyes and hands wandered down to unbutton Brianna's pants. They undressed one another fervently. Kissing. Touching. Rubbing. Pam felt her heart pounding in her chest as Brianna planted kisses all over her body. It was like being drenched after a drought. When she tasted Brianna's lips against hers, it was as if she were being fed after famine, finding her breath after being buried. The concert of emotions made her body come alive. She whimpered as Brianna's warm mouth took to her breasts. Sucking. Holding. Caressing. Pam's legs trembled as Brianna roamed her body, adorning her womanly attributes with kisses. She was beside herself with ecstasy and pleasure and closed her eyes. Pam submerged herself in the bliss. She had waited more than a decade for this.

Brianna loved how smooth Pam's body felt as she glided her hands against Pam's skin. Her fingers passed over the beautiful curves delicately and with care. Pam's moans were a melody to Brianna's ears. High and low. Fast-paced and then long and drawn out. Soft and strong. A steady waver. Pam was a symphony under

Brianna's direction. She guided her tongue to the center of Pam's gorgeous body, grazing over her most sensitive area that was begging for Brianna's full attention. She kissed it softly but did not linger. Not yet. She wanted the experience to last too. She toured Pam's body with intrigue and affection, as if it were a radiant dream on an endless night. Brianna was chivalrous with her exploration. She kissed all the way down to Pam's feet before returning to the core of her femininity.

Pam gripped Brianna's shoulders, uncontrollably thrusting upward the instant she felt Brianna tasting her. She sighed deeply. Gratefully.

"Brianna…" Pam had lost her words. "Mmm…" She was wading in euphoria.

Brianna's tongue bathed in the river formed at crux Pam's womanhood, slipping inside to tour the sweet velvet walls of her essence. She dove deep. Reaching. Sliding in and out. Probing. Kissing. Brianna was a willing slave to Pam's flesh and would not rest until she had given Pam complete satisfaction. She moved to the beat of the pounding between her own legs, continuing until Pam reached a screaming climax that was muted by one of the pillows. Somehow she had remembered to be cautious in the heat of the moment. Brianna was grateful because she had clumsily forgotten to think what her neighbors might imagine if they heard a woman screaming her name at the height of an incredible orgasm. She exhaled in sudden relief and from exhaustion. Brianna needed a few moments to pace herself. Her body was on the edge of release from the enjoyment of pleasing Pam, but she couldn't let that happen prematurely. That would be terrible.

"Oh my God," was all Pam could whisper when Brianna lay beside her. "Brianna…" she had to catch her breath before going on.

Pam's heart was still beating hurriedly and the pulse between her legs had just begun to soften and slow. She shivered when Brianna placed her hand on her stomach. Unable to complete her thoughts with words, Pam kissed Brianna. She kissed her forehead, her nose, and her lips. They lay facing one another, so close they shared air. What Pam breathed out, Brianna breathed in. Pam reached for Brianna's hands, intertwining their fingers. The shadows of candles danced about in the room as they lay still. Words weren't needed. A blanket of rapture formed above them, and they were covered in pleasure.

Losing Control

Eventually Pam climbed on top of Brianna. The heat they traded was electrifying. Pam reciprocated the attention she'd received from Brianna. She stroked Brianna's body with a gentle tongue and soft lips to the point of a bursting climax.

The night wore on with repeated episodes of passion until the sheets were damp from perspiration and the air was clouded with the scent of sex.

Chapter 22

The next morning, as Pam slept, Brianna looked at her with great endearment. The sun had not risen yet, but Brianna had awakened with a smile stretched across her face. She watched the slight up and down movement of Pam's abdomen as she breathed, admiring Pam as she lay in a pleasant slumber. Brianna's mind spun with colorful fantasies of what joy lay ahead for both of them. She was still feeling the intoxication from the previous evening's sexual indulgence. She sighed. Brianna could drink a dozen cases of Pam and not feel guilty of gluttony.

She placed a soft kiss on Pam's cheek, and Pam stirred in response. A half-grin formed on her face. The moment felt like a dream. The room was still and dark. Visions of a life that she and Pam could have filled Brianna's mind. She became so ensconced in daydreams that she did not realize when Pam had awakened by her side.

"Deep in thought?" Pam asked. Sleep was written all over her face, but to Brianna, she was still a wonder. Still a beauty.

Brianna grinned bashfully. "I guess so."

"I hope they were pleasant."

"Definitely." Brianna used her thumb to trace the shape of Pam's eyebrows. She held Pam's face and stared at her as if she were looking into the eyes of a goddess. "Definitely good thoughts."

The two women lay in bed together replaying the events from the evening before, first in conversation and then in action. They enjoyed each other's body again…and again…and again.

Losing Control

Hours later, Brianna finally slid out of bed to retrieve a bathrobe and a spare one for Pam. They needed to get up and replenish the energy they'd spent on each other. After giving Pam a new guest set of toiletries, Brianna went to the kitchen to cut fresh fruit to serve her for breakfast. She hummed the entire time. The morning was just as fulfilling as the night before. They enjoyed each other's company, basking in the afterglow of the joining of their bodies and minds. They only became saddened when Pam said she had to go.

"I'll call you later."

"All right." Brianna didn't want to show too much disappointment. "I'll be waiting."

Pam said she and Eric needed to get a move on figuring out their separation, and she wanted to be there when he got home to bring it up. Brianna understood and hoped the process would go as quickly as possible. She recognized that it wouldn't happen overnight. *Just be patient.*

Traces of Pam lingered long after she had departed. Her scent had been pressed into the sheets, and her image had burned into Brianna's mind. What a night!

The days passed with progress. November wound down to make way for December and Brianna was content and happy for the first time in a long time. All was well until she got a mid-month phone call from Pam. The two words that fell from Pam's lips were heavy enough to sink a ship.

"I'm pregnant."

Brianna couldn't organize the bedlam in her mind fast enough to summon a thoughtful response. She was in shock and utterly confused. "What?"

"I don't know how it happened, Brianna. Eric is sterile. At least that what we've always thought…" Pam's voice trailed off into nothingness. The words hurt too much to speak aloud, scraping her throat on their painful passage.

Pam and Eric had been living separately for a few weeks, and Brianna and Pam had being seeing each other consistently. Brianna had fallen in love with Pam. Pam loved her too. Eric's lack of fertility was not a surprise to Brianna. Pam had already told her that in one of their many late-night conversations. They spoke every night and saw each other whenever they could, but for the last week Pam hadn't been feeling well. She was constantly nauseous and tired. She felt an onslaught of headaches, sometimes dizzying her. She'd chalked it all up to stress until she missed her menstrual cycle, but then she thought stress may have caused that as well.

Unable to stand the changes in her body and at the behest of Brianna, she'd gone to the doctor to find out what was wrong. Just to cover all the bases, her doctor had told her she should take a pregnancy test. Pam had been treated by the same physician for years and was surprised at the request but complied. She knew it would come back negative. Pam had not missed a period in fifteen years. This was just a fluke. She was actually looking forward to her period going away for good! She was in her early forties and menopause should have been quickly approaching. Good riddance. Maybe this *was* menopause, she'd thought!

The notion of pregnancy seemed unreal, but she unwillingly recalled the last time she'd had sex with Eric. It had been during a fleeting moment that she tried to appease him days before the election. She hadn't even participated. Pam had laid there and let Eric have her in a twisted attempt to bring them closer together again. Her mind couldn't have been further away from him while he mated with her. Her skin seemed to crawl in disgust under his touch. They could never be *normal* again she thought. She was annoyed with herself for even making such a stupid attempt and counted the minutes until he finished. The positive test results nearly made Pam faint.

"Does he know?" Brianna asked. She knew that at one time Pam did want children of her own but got accustomed to not having any around.

"No." Pam's hand shook as she held the phone close to her ear. "I have to tell him though, don't I?"

Brianna was silent. Did she? Yes, deep down Brianna knew the right thing to do was to tell Eric, but what would that mean for *her*? Searing tears streamed down her cheeks. She was afraid. "I—I guess you do. It's only fair." She couldn't bring herself to advise Pam to withhold that type of information from Eric. It was just too selfish.

The phone line was quiet.

179

"What do you want to do, Pam? Do you want to keep it?"

Questions exploded in Pam's mind. Did she want to keep it? Was this pregnancy God's intervention? Would she be stealing from Eric if she aborted? Abortion? Could she live with herself after having an abortion? She felt another headache coming on. "I don't know," she mumbled. But the true answer was blasting inside of her even though she didn't want to acknowledge it. She wanted to keep the baby.

Brianna felt cheated. Just when she'd opened herself up enough to fall in a love with a woman, she was in jeopardy of having that woman snatched away from her, as if she had never been the rightful owner in the first place. Anguish drained her. Not only did she love Pam, she would have to work with Pam for the next couple of years. "When do you plan to tell him?" she asked. The question was a bushel of thorns dragging against her throat.

"Soon. I have to tell him soon."

Somehow Brianna *knew* things would not be happily ever after. She was caught in a maelstrom of grief. This baby was bad news. She felt horrible for her self-centered thought but couldn't help it.

"How do you think he's going to react?" Brianna's mouth went dry as she spoke.

"I don't know." Pam's response was hushed. Nervousness devoured her as her world seemed to pick up a strong sense of urgency. "I should get in touch with him now. The sooner the better."

Brianna felt as if she'd just been slapped in the face. "Okay…call me back, please."

"Of course, baby." Pam was near tears, trying to be soothing with her choice of words. She knew Brianna must be in a pool of her own despair.

"All right."

They hung up without a goodbye. For Brianna, life seemed to screech to a heart-wrenching stop. *Baby,* the affectionate name rang in her ears. Why did this have to happen! She felt sucked into a tunnel of uncertainty. Inhaling rank reality and choking on the smell, Brianna felt suffocated by dark clouds of what-ifs. What if this and what if that. She was sick of what-ifs. She wanted predictability. She wanted stability.

Cheril N. Clarke

"Please don't let us be over…" She spoke aloud to herself. She closed her eyes and tried to control her unruly mind from berating her with *I told you so*. Things would be okay. *Relax*. Brianna kept telling herself not to worry. She needed to calm down.

Pam dialed Eric's cell phone number with trembling fingers. Her heart pounded as she listened to his phone ring. Just when she was preparing to leave him a message, he picked up.

"Pamela?" he answered. He sounded annoyed. She could hear a paging system in the background. He was at an airport. The noisy background was familiar to her.

"Yes, it's me."

"What is it?"

"Eric, I need to talk to you. Actually, I need to see you. It's important." She couldn't tell him the news over the phone.

"What's so important that you need to see me?"

"You sound like you're at an airport. When are you coming back from your trip?" She ignored his inquiry, speaking nervously.

"I'm just getting back. What do you want?" he spat.

"I have something to tell you, but I don't want to do it over the phone."

Eric walked outside and hailed a taxi. "Why not? I'm busy." He just didn't want to see her. He tossed his things in the cab and slid into the back seat.

"Eric, *please*." A tear glided down her left cheek.

He huffed. "I can come by the house tonight."

"Can you come now?" she pushed.

"Where to?" the African cab driver interrupted.

"Twenty-three hundred Walnut Street. Thanks." Eric had sublet an apartment from a colleague until he and Pam worked things out with their separation and divorce. He lived closer to his job in Philadelphia now.

"Please?" Pam pleaded.

"What is going on with you?" Her whining incensed him. She used to be his refuge after spending days on the road, but now she just added to the stress of living out of a suitcase. She was like a mosquito in his ear.

"Would you just come over, please!" The words fell from her lips without hesitation.

"All right. All right. I'll be there soon." Eric hung up. He would go see her to get rid of her. "Change of plans," he spoke to the driver.

"What's that?"

"Take me to Jersey, please. I'll direct you once we get across the Walt Whitman Bridge."

Eric leaned back against the seat with his eyes closed. What the hell did Pam want?

When Eric arrived at the home he used to share with Pam, disdain pricked his skin. She opened the door the moment she saw the taxi pull up. Eric looked sharp as usual, wearing a black wool coat that was unbuttoned and a midnight blue suit with a celery green silk tie. His wedding band shined in the sunlight. She didn't know he was still wearing it and suddenly felt guilty for removing hers already. Was he still holding on to hope? She didn't think he would at this point. He seemed to hate her now. The symbol confused her. Eric took his small suitcase from the car and pulled it behind him as he walked toward her.

She stepped aside to let him in. "Do you want something to drink?"

"What do you want?" Eric didn't sit down.

So much for easing into it, she thought. "I...I um—" Pam stuttered, struggling to find the right words. She began to cry. "Oh, Eric!"

"Pamela, what is the matter?" She was starting to alarm him with her theatrics. He hated that he still even cared about her. Why wasn't she crying to Brianna? "I'm leaving if you don't start talking."

Pam leaned against the island in their kitchen, resting her face on her balled-up fists. She sniffled. "I went to the doctor today..."

"And?" His eyes met hers.

"And..."

He exhaled impatiently.

"And I found out that I'm pregnant."

Eric chuckled. He wasn't even sure if he'd heard her right, he didn't know how else to respond. "What are you telling me for? You and I both know that it can't be mine."

"You're the only man I've been with since we've been together, Eric." She looked at him through eyes reddened with sorrow.

"You expect me to believe that?" He was angry now. "You were the one fucking around on me, Pam! I can't make babies. It's not mine!" Eric was furious.

"God damn it. It *has* to be! I swear on my life that I have *never* slept with another man during our marriage!" She was reeling from his response.

"Bullshit!"

"It's the truth!"

Eric rolled his eyes. "Get a second opinion or find the man who you fucked to get knocked up because it damn sure ain't mine!" His voice was raw and rancid with disgust. Eric was crushed. She had slept with another man! What a bitch! He didn't want to believe it, but how could he not? How could he trust anything out of her mouth after he'd caught her lying before? His stomach recoiled in rage. Eric grabbed his luggage, ready to leave. "I don't believe this shit. I gotta get out of here." He had to get away from her. He had to leave *now*.

Pam pulled at his arm. "Wait! Don't walk away from me!"

"Pam, if you don't—" he stopped speaking in effort to avoid feeding his anger. He yanked himself from her grip as if her fingertips were poison.

Pam took a step back. "The doctor tested me twice. I'm pregnant. I don't know if it's God's intervention or what, but this baby is yours." She placed her hands on her belly, still trying to grasp the fact that there was a life growing inside of her. "It's yours…"

Eric's eyes reluctantly followed her hands and the fierce wrinkles in his forehead seem to loosen a bit. A part of him had real concern that she was lying, and another part of him heard only one word: God. Could it be? He was never really religious, but Eric always accepted that there were things in life that didn't have an explanation. Could this be one of them? "I want a paternity test to prove it's mine," he demanded coldly. Turmoil overpowered his brief wonder of divine intervention.

Losing Control

Pam felt struck by his words. A waterfall of tears sprang from here eyes, blurring her vision. She had to sit down. The stress was too much. "What? Are you serious? We can't get one of those right now, not until the baby is born." She broke down and began to bawl. "Eric, I'm not lying, and I can't do this alone," she heard herself say. "I don't want to abort it."

Eric stared at her. It ate away at him to see her so distraught, and the suggestion of abortion didn't sit right with him. Suddenly the possibility of fatherhood became more real. What if he wasn't sterile after all? Eric finally took off his coat and sat down. He cleared his throat and loosened his tie. He felt sweat building on his skin. He looked at Pam intently. Studying her. Deep down he didn't think she had been with another man, but he had to be sure. "We'll do a paternity test," he said with finality. "If it's mine you know I'll take care of it. I'm a man and no matter what happened between us, I would not abandon my child…*if* it's mine." The last three words almost caught in his throat. Could he really be a father? Eric rubbed his forehead, trying to digest the situation.

Pam only wept.

Chapter 23

Frank was worried about Brianna. He sat stiffly in a chair while Terrence cut his hair. Two months had gone by, and Eric still wanted nothing to do with Pam until his paternity could be proven. Brianna had stepped up, accompanying Pam to her doctor's visits, and their love for each other had grown despite the circumstances. Things were trying, to say the least. Brianna had been sworn in and was officially a member of city council. Though she was thrilled to have accomplished her goal, her personal life was still in disorder, and Frank was concerned about Brianna's state of mind. He sighed, wishing there was something that he could do to make her feel better.

"Send her some flowers, man." Terrence knew why Frank was sitting in the chair so quietly.

"What?"

"No matter what's wrong," Terrence said as he perfected his cut. "Flowers will cheer her up. At least for a little while."

Frank wasn't sure if the gesture was appropriate.

"Send them as a friend, not as her man," he instructed. The words came out a little stronger than he intended. "They'll make her feel better." Terrence only hoped that one day someone would be so concerned about him.

"With what kind of card?"

"I don't know. Just say something like, 'You'll make it through,' or something like that."

"All right. I'll do that."

Terrence tilted Frank's head back to give him a close shave. Frank's attention to Brianna generated envy in Terrence, but he pushed the feeling aside. They were all friends now. *Just friends.*

"Why don't you come over there with me?" Frank asked.

"To Brianna's?" Terrence was shocked by the question.

"Yeah, let's surprise her. The flowers will be from us instead of just me."

Terrence thought about it and smiled. "Okay."

"Cool."

That evening they arrived at Brianna's condo with a large floral arrangement in tow.

"Hey!" She smiled broadly when she opened the door, gasping when she saw the flowers Terrence was holding.

"Hey, yourself," Frank said. He gave her a hug.

"Come on in."

"These are for you," Terrence said and handed them to her.

"Aw." She beamed. "Thank you, guys!"

Terrence was right. The gift had a great impact on Brianna. When Frank had stopped by to see her the night before, she was extremely sad. Pam was away for the weekend, and Brianna was sitting at home miserable on a Saturday night.

"You're welcome. We hope you like them," Frank said.

"I do. Thank you so much!" There was a glimmer of happiness in her eyes. She took the vase and placed it on her dining room table.

"Now that's what we want to see tonight," Terrence said. "I know you have a lot on your mind but tonight just try to have some fun, okay? We brought some liquor and some board games to take your mind off things."

"Board games?" Brianna asked. She hadn't had a games night in ages!

"Yes, so stop all of that crying and get drunk, girl!"

Frank laughed uncomfortably. He still had to get used to some of Terrence's mannerisms. Terrence was by no means overtly feminine, but he did have certain behaviors, ones he only displayed around them, that were telltale signs that he was gay.

"Well, all right," Brianna said. "But I can't stay up all night or get too drunk. Neither should y'all. Everybody has to work in the morning."

"Excuse me, but I'm my *own* boss," Terrence interjected.

They shared a laugh and relaxed. The evening was good for Brianna. She was happy to have Frank and Terrence come by and calm the storm. Their friendship was truly valued.

Eric's nerves were rattled. He had avoided Pam since the day she had told him she was pregnant, but his feelings were ripping him apart. He was angry and bitter, yet as the days wore on, he had become curious. He wondered more and more about the baby and if he were the father. When he couldn't stand it anymore, he went to the doctor. He wanted to know the odds of misdiagnosis and the possibility of fatherhood for him. When he spoke with his physician, Eric's world was shaken.

"It's not completely impossible, Eric," his doctor said.

"But—"

"You have a low sperm count. Even though the chances of getting your wife pregnant are slim, it's not impossible."

"Yeah, but Doc…"

His doctor looked at him with sympathetic eyes. "It's possible," he repeated.

Eric sighed. "All right. Thanks."

Tepid excitement crept into his belly, almost broiled in the caldron of resentment that had been brewing for Pam. The baby might be his! Howls of protest fought thoughts of wonder. Love collided with hate and joy and clawed at pain. Eric had never felt so conflicted in his life. He admitted to himself that he didn't really think Pam had slept with another man, but he would make her go through the test anyway. He was too stubborn to withdraw his request. It made him feel like he had *some* power.

Even though Pam enraged Eric, a piece of him was still with her. And now, he realized, that a piece of him may literally still be with her—growing inside of her. How would they parent? He didn't want his child around Brianna at all. Pam would not raise his baby around that lifestyle. He wouldn't have it. He didn't want another

Losing Control

man in Pam's life either. Eric wrestled with his feelings. *We have to get back together*, he thought.

Chapter 24

"Are you sure you can't get a test done before the baby is born?" Eric asked over the phone.

Pam got out of the bed, leaving Brianna alone. "I can, but I could lose the baby, Eric. I'm not willing to take that chance." She was tired of him. One minute he cared, the next he didn't. It was too early in the morning for her to deal with him.

"Lose the baby?"

"Yes, I've told you that already!"

"Oh," he lamented. He didn't remember her saying that. "Don't do it then." He realized he couldn't handle taking that chance either. His stubbornness on the topic began to yield. He ran his hands over his face. "But I still want you to get the other tests done. We'll check the baby after you have it."

"Excuse me? For what?"

Brianna stared at Pam as she spoke into the phone. Pam didn't want to take the call outside of the room, but felt awkward speaking to him with Brianna so close by. She felt disrespectful and didn't know what she should have done. She couldn't ignore him.

Eric couldn't help himself. "I don't know who you've else been with or how far you've gotten into that lifestyle. I want to be sure you're still healthy."

"Fuck you, Eric. You're out of your mind." Pam finally walked out of the room. "You should know I've only been with one other person."

"*I'm* out of my mind? All I'm saying that if that's my baby I want to know that you're taking care of yourself."

"I am taking care of myself, okay? I have a clean bill of health and the only thing wrong with me is the fact that I'm stuck carrying a piece of you!"

Her words blindsided him.

Pam continued. "While you were in denial, I was sure to go to all of my doctors appointments and do everything I needed to do for my baby so don't even insult me like that!" Eric had pissed her off. "You know what? I can't deal with this shit." He was giving her a headache and she was already emotional. Granted, he had a right to be upset, but he was so mean to her. She couldn't take it at that moment. At the same time, she couldn't help but think she deserved his treatment. What if he had cheated on her? Would she be as understanding as she expected him to be?

"I'm still your husband."

"For now."

"Maybe forever. If you think you're going to raise my baby with Brianna you're mistaken."

"That's not your decision."

"Yes, it is."

"No, it's not!" Pam grieved. "You're stressing me out."

Brianna walked into the living room. She gave Pam a look that told her she should get off the phone.

"I'm sorry, Pam." Eric lightened up.

"Whatever." Pam hung up.

"Are you okay?" Brianna walked closer to her. "Come on and sit down."

Pam started to cry. "I'm sorry, Brianna."

"Shh. Just relax." Brianna put her anger aside and tried to assuage Pam.

"I just don't know what to do."

Brianna was silent. She wanted to be careful in choosing her words.

"Did you hear me, baby?" Pam questioned.

"Yeah," Brianna spoke quietly. Though she'd only heard one side of Pam's conversation, she'd heard enough to be livid. She was disgusted with Eric's puerile behavior and did her best to help Pam find solace amidst the gust of emotions rattling their situation. Through it all, Brianna wondered who would comfort her.

Brianna and Pam had talked extensively as the weeks went by. It was clear that Pam was torn. Even though she had no desire to stay married to Eric, she was terrified of raising the baby with Brianna.

"I don't think I'm strong enough to be a gay parent, Bri," she'd said one night.

"Don't worry about being gay, just be a parent." Brianna was afraid of where Pam's thoughts were going. "Protect your child and love your child. Nurture and teach your child," she added.

"It's not that easy. Not for me at least." She spoke quietly, unsure of herself.

Brianna had to keep reminding herself that Pam still struggled with self-loathing and feeling like a sinner for living as a lesbian. "I didn't say it would be easy, but do you think raising it alone would be easier?"

"I would have Eric."

Uppercut. Pam's response was a powerful blow. "You'd go back to him after the way he's been treating you?"

"Maybe I deserved it."

"You did not!" Brianna moved away from Pam and looked at her sharply.

Things were tense. Another miscalculated thought of Pam's spoken aloud would ignite Brianna.

"Okay," Brianna paused to gather herself. "You did cheat on him emotionally. You did break your vows to him, but did he have to be as cruel as he's been?"

Pam was silent.

"He's a fucking asshole!" The words barreled out of Brianna's mouth with fury. "You want to go back to a man who shoved you into a wall? Cursed you out like a dog? He never even went to the obstetrician with you when you told him you were pregnant with *his* child!" She was blinded by her pain, incapable of seeing Eric's side. "He treated you like shit!"

"He's been angry, Brianna! *I* did wrong. *I* broke his heart."

"Yeah, well what about mine, Pam!" Brianna burst into tears. She couldn't believe Pam was defending Eric. "What about my heart!" Her words were marred by her cries. She buried her face in her hands.

"Bri…" Pam moved closer to Brianna. "Baby, don't cry. Please…"

Jealousy stormed through Brianna. She knew this might happen. She knew it all along!

"I'm sorry, Brianna. Please, babe. You know I didn't mean to hurt you. I never wanted to hurt you, Brianna, but you knew—" Pam clipped her words before they turned into statements that would further harm Brianna. "I'm sorry," she repeated, and hugged Brianna tightly. Pam felt Brianna tremble as she sobbed in her arms. "I'm so sorry. I…" Pam lost her words as tears began to fill her eyes too. Had she broken Brianna's heart too? The pain was unbearable. "I don't know what I'm going to do."

Brianna couldn't force Pam to stay with her. She couldn't talk Pam out of sacrificing herself for what she *thought* was the best for the child. And yes, she knew that things might get bad before they got good, but she could have never predicted how strong the hurt would be. Brianna had never had her heart broken before. The feeling was new.

"I didn't say I was going back to him," Pam whispered and kissed Brianna's forehead. She tried to soothe her. "Let's just stop and not get ahead of ourselves."

Silence. Brianna's thoughts were torture. She felt like she would die from her self-inflicted wounds. Why didn't she listen to her mind instead of her heart! Hot tears streamed down her face.

"I love you, Brianna. Just give me time to sort things out," Pam pleaded. "I just need a little more time."

Brianna cried quietly, giving no response. Only raw endurance of the heart would be able to measure the time that Pam needed. *Walk away before it gets even worse.* Brianna felt trapped. *Run away!* She didn't know what to do either. Was it safer to retreat or remain? Which would hurt less in the long run? It had been clear from the beginning that Pam might not be the anodyne her lonely heart had been craving, but she had partaken of Pam anyway. The situation had grated her to pieces.

"Baby, please don't cry." Pam kissed her again. She brushed the hair away from Brianna's brow and pulled her closer. It was her turn to be strong.

Cheril N. Clarke

"What am *I* supposed to do?" Brianna questioned. She knew Pam didn't have the answer. She cried.

Chapter 25

Burdened by guilt of ruining of her marriage and tired of fighting with Eric compelled Pam to eventually give in to his request for medical testing, including tests for all STDs. She felt obligated, as if she owed him that much after lying to him.

"Pam, you're in excellent health." Her doctor spoke definitively, handing her a paper with an explanation of her tests.

"Thank you." Pam quickly turned to walk out, throwing the document at Eric on her way out. Her face was flushed with embarrassment.

She felt as though her life had turned into an episode of trashy daytime television. She suddenly felt weak, unstable. Her heart was bleeding from the pain.

Eric stuffed the paperwork in his pocket and went after her. "Pam, wait!"

"Get away from me!" she shouted when Eric approached her.

"But Pam..." All of the hurt that he'd flung upon Pam boomeranged at him with an arctic chill. He knew that his demands would hurt Pam, but didn't realize how the pain and humiliation in her eyes would impale him too. He wished he could take it all back, but it was too late. Eric was overcome with emotion. He was speechless.

Still shattered from his degradation, Pam walked to her car without a word, only a steady flow of tears. She had no STDs! Her insides crumbled under the weight of his accusations. Eric's cruelty had beaten her to the ground and doused her with shame.

He wondered what he could do to pull her from the sea of sorrow that she was drowning in—the murky waters that he'd thrown her in with his callous behavior. Regret began to swell his throat.

Pam sobbed until she shook, leaning against her vehicle. Her head was aching and she felt dizzy with emotion. She wanted to see Brianna badly and she wanted to be away from Eric.

"Pam?" Eric called her again. He pulled her close to him and squeezed her in his arms. She did not move.

Pam stood with her arms dangling by her side as if she had no life. But there was life. *This* was life. And she didn't know what to do next.

"Just leave me alone, Eric!" Pam screamed. They were at their house and he was pestering her with apologies and questions. Eric had made an about-face!

"Pam, please talk to me!"

She stormed away from him and closed herself in the master bedroom. She wanted Brianna. It didn't feel right with him there. It was as if the house were under a large shadow. Nothing was as it should be. Everything felt *wrong*.

Go away, she thought, as she heard him coming up the stairs. *Just go away, PLEASE!* Pam lay in the bed curled in fetal position. All of the pain made her feel less than alive.

Eric entered the room and sat at the edge of the bed. "I'm sorry, Pam. Can we talk?" He paused. "Please?"

"I have nothing to say to you."

He sighed. "Can you just listen to me then?"

Pam groaned in annoyance. "I'd rather not."

The silence after her response was deafening. Timidly, Eric reached around her and placed his hand on her stomach. Before he could rest his hand on the bump in her belly for longer than a second Pam moved away from him.

"Don't touch me!" Pam began crying again.

Losing Control

Eric pulled her back to him and hugged her. When she fought him off, he did not let go. When she cursed him, he did not let go. When she bawled, he squeezed her tighter. Things had changed and he had accepted that the baby was his. He couldn't hate her. The only other option was to love her.

Chapter 26

Everything was a fight. Doing her job was a fight. Talking to Pam was a battle. Finding peace was a war. At a time in her career that she needed to excel the most, Brianna struggled. She was ill-equipped but tried to survive with what she had. Sheldon was still around to provide strength, guidance and advice for work, but that was it. Her only refuge from the torrential rains in her life was her friendship with Terrence and Frank. Brianna still saw Pam. She had to deal with her every now and again for work. Each look into Pam's eyes was a spear in Brianna's heart. Despite her greatest effort, the love she had for Pam was inextinguishable. It was constant combat just to keep her tears away.

Brianna had decided to pull back. As Pam's belly got bigger and things got more dramatic she realized that she couldn't compete with Eric. She didn't want to try. It was bad timing. If she failed at work and made a fool of herself in office she'd never be re-elected. She needed to focus. Brianna couldn't throw all of her hard work away. She had to work through the heartbreak, paying dearly for her poor judgment.

Pam begged. She pleaded. She didn't want to lose Brianna but couldn't satisfy her *and* Eric. Brianna wanted out and Eric wanted in. To Pam, it seemed like the only way to clean up her mess was for her to give them both what they wanted and forget about herself. She had caused great pain for all of them and had trouble forgiving herself. All she did was blame herself and cry. She couldn't remember the last time she smiled. Her pregnancy was a catastrophe. Sometimes she wondered if she should have aborted and chosen herself, but it was too late now. The window had closed.

Things would never be the same. She didn't want to be married, but found it difficult to go forward with a divorce. Brianna had given up on her, and though it hurt, Pam understood. She had no idea how they could be just friends, but wanted to try. Wishful thinking. They were never just friends so how could they go back to that? Brianna had made that point and it rang loudly in Pam's ears. Depression tugged at Pam from every angle, so much so that Eric fussed over her even more. He was worried about her and the stress on the baby. She didn't want to eat. She worked and slept, that was it: a bitter cycle. Pam barely spoke to him. She only clung to memories, holding on for dear life to the few months of bliss she'd had with Brianna. The recollections were her only friend.

Eric began going to anger management classes. He went on his own. Acknowledgement of his child—a girl, had changed him. He was eternally sorry for his abuse of Pam. He regretted every hurtful thing that he'd ever said and wished he could go back in time to fix the night that he'd shoved her in anger. He was sorry. Eric had a psychotherapist too. He wanted to be a good man again. Somehow he'd lost his way, but he was making a genuine effort to be the best husband that he could be despite everything that happened. It wouldn't be easy. He worked through his hurt, even when it blazed inside of him, trying to prod Pam along but she only went through motions of daily life.

Pam was more a zombie than a woman. Not only did she barely speak to him. She refused to sleep with him. The closest to affection he'd gotten was when she allowed him to rest his head on her belly to experience the baby. The baby was the thread holding them together. Sometimes he thought he saw a spark of the Pam he married in her eyes when something significant happened, like getting the sonogram done, but it disappeared before fully forming. She was just a shell. Emotionless. When he kissed her stomach she winced. Her reaction stabbed him. Eric had slain a part of her in his battle to hurt her more than she had hurt him and now everything felt wrong.

Eric wanted to fix things. He hoped they would heal in time. They *had* to. If he could forgive her infidelity then surely she could forgive his reaction to it. When he was at a loss as to what to do he just loved her. Even when she ignored him, he kept trying. He worked on his pain in therapy and tried to work on hers at home. He cooked. He cleaned. He got her whatever she wanted when she wanted it, even when she didn't ask him to. He even began traveling less for work. He made changes and he made sacrifices. He had no idea if any of it would be worth it, but he held on to hope. He wanted his family. Through everything that Eric had gone through, he'd learned that love was something you *do* not something you *have*.

Chapter 27

Seven months into her pregnancy, Pam felt herself on the edge of a deep depression. She was sick of Eric and wanted to be free of him. Her doctor and Eric were very worried about her. Eric, however, tried to keep his distance because he knew it was him who was making her sink to new lows. He pulled back and gave her space.

One evening after working late Pam found herself driving to Brianna's condo. They hadn't spoken to each other outside of work in a few weeks, but not a day had gone by that Pam didn't think of Brianna. Pam didn't know what possessed her to drop by unannounced, but before she knew it she was pulling into a visitor's space, parking right next to Brianna's silver Genesis Coupe. *She's home.* Anxiety filled Pam as she reached in her purse for her cell phone. Tears began to build in her eyes as she dialed Brianna's number.

"Hello?"

There was a dead silence on the phone line. Pam lost her courage.

"Pam." Brianna knew it was her from the caller ID. Her heart skipped a beat.

Pam sniffled. "Yeah," she spoke softly. "It's me. Please, can I come up?"

Brianna took off her reading glasses and put down the novel she was immersed in. She sat up in her bed. "What? You're here?"

"Yes."

"Um. Okay then. Yeah, come on up." Brianna rubbed her forehead. She wasn't dressed for company, but didn't have the energy to change. She opened the door wearing a pink and grey cotton loungewear set from Victoria's Secret.

Once face to face, the women stood awkwardly, finding it difficult to look into each other's eyes.

"Come in," Brianna said.

Pam entered and Brianna closed the door behind her.

"Is everything okay?"

"I'm sorry for just dropping by like this. I don't know what got into me. I just had to see you. I needed to be near you. I miss you. Brianna—"

"Pam." Brianna lowered her head and stared at the floor. She couldn't take this. She'd actually gone the whole day without dwelling on Pam or in the hole in her heart.

"Wait. Just wait. Please, just let me say whatever it is I came here to say." Pam reached for Brianna's hand.

Reluctantly, Brianna let her fingers intertwine with Pam's. Tears began to creep into the corner of Brianna's eyes as she looked at Pam, filled with growing life. She felt torn, wishing the baby never existed yet marveling at the beauty of Pam as she stood there carrying another being inside of her. Brianna wanted to touch Pam's belly, but then again she did not. She wiped a tear from her eye before it could fall.

They went and sat down on the couch.

"I need you in my life," Pam began. The words fell from her lips before she could finish thinking them through.

Brianna listened.

"I thought I could go back to living a lie. I thought everything would eventually work itself out if I gave both you and Eric what you wanted," she said and looked Brianna in her eyes. "But I was wrong. I'm dying inside. I miss you. I need you."

"But how—"

"I don't know how, but I have to have you."

"What about Eric?"

"I can't stand him."

"And the baby?"

"She's mine…and his, but that doesn't mean he and I have to stay with him to raise her." Pam's hand trembled as she spoke. "I'll just have to be strong enough to make the best decision for me. No matter what, the baby will be well taken care of. So that just leaves me."

Brianna didn't want to be a fool again. She didn't want to take her heart through the wringer again, but it was already palpitating while listening to Pam speak. "I don't think I can handle this, Pam."

"I know I hurt you, and I'm sorry. I never meant to. Sometimes I wish I would have never approached you that day, but I did. And being with you made me get honest with myself." She moved closer to Brianna on the couch. "I know it's asking a lot, but I have to at least try one last time. Please, can we work on *our* relationship?"

"We're not in a relationship." Brianna felt as if she were in a dream. Was this really happening?

"Then would you consider getting in one with me? I'm ready to end things with Eric. I mean it. I want a divorce." Pam placed a hand on Brianna's knee and cupped her face with her other hand. "I love you."

Brianna was silent, wrestling with her feelings.

"Are you going to make a pregnant woman get on her knees and beg?" Pam stood up and began to kneel. "I'll get down, but I might need some help getting back up," she joked.

"Oh, stop it!" Brianna laughed finally. The tension had been broken and the mood was somewhat lightened. She pulled Pam back on the couch.

"Please," Pam pleaded.

"I don't know what to say!"

"Say you'll think about it. Say you won't walk away from me when I need you. Tell me if you love me too."

The moment got serious again.

"I do," Brianna stared at her. "I do love you, Pamela Thompson."

"Griffin," Pam corrected.

"What?"

"Griffin. It's my maiden name."

There was a silence in the room after Pam spoke. Her cell phone cut right through it, however. She ignored the call without looking to see who it was.

"Griffin, huh?"

"Yes."

Brianna pulled Pam close to her and held her in an embrace. "I'll think about it," she whispered and began to weep silently. "That's all I can do right now."

"That's all I'm asking." Pam kissed Brianna on her neck.

"Please…" Brianna moaned. She wanted to fight the urge to ride the wave of emotions present.

Pam kissed her again and Brianna felt a flutter in her stomach.

Brianna couldn't fight it. "I missed you," she said softly, and began to plant kisses of her own.

Pam turned her phone off to quiet it from ringing and lost herself in the evening. She was where *she* wanted to be. Fear rushed through Brianna at lightning speed, but she ignored it. She was with who she wanted to be with. She was terrified deep down inside, but couldn't stop the night.

Their conversation was quickly taken over by their longing for one another and they ended up making delicate love. While Brianna's intensity was as strong as a lion, her touch was as soft as silk. She carefully caressed Pam's every curve, massaging away her pain with brushes and kisses of endearment. She loved Pam slowly, appreciating every second of their exchange of energy. Overwhelmed, Pam's climax came with tears of rapture.

They enjoyed each other until they both lay with teary eyes and in each other's arms. Pam was afraid, but ready to live for herself.

Losing Control

Epilogue

    Brianna drove with the windows down, feeling a warm summer breeze against her face as she headed north on the New Jersey turnpike. The days were long and they were hard. She didn't want to live without Pam, but found being with her an incredulous battle. Their relationship was a secret to all but those who found out during the race. It would be too big of a scandal to let anyone else know. They had only gotten one foot out of the closet, just enough to let a draft of air inside so they could breath easier. Pam did file for a divorce, but her separation with Eric was bound to be treacherous. He moved out again and Pam was alone in their house. She considered taking out a restraining order on him because she was afraid of what he might do but was more concerned about the possibility of her personal life becoming public knowledge in a negative light. Eric had controlled his anger in their fights, but Pam never forgot the time when he couldn't. She never would and with emotions running as high as they were she was afraid Eric might snap. She prayed he didn't.
    A month had passed since Pam and Brianna had the talk about their future and Pam was expecting to deliver the baby within the coming weeks. She was excited and scared. Eric was bitter and angry, yet had a strange beam of light in his eyes when they managed to be civil to one another and talk about their baby. He was torn and often looked as though he were fighting tears. Brianna needed a break from it all. She needed to get away to clear her mind and regroup. She had no idea how things would play out with Pam, Eric and the baby, but she couldn't bring herself to leave Pam alone. They did not live together, but they spent every free minute they had with each other. Love held them together.
    Brianna struggled onward, trying her best to manage her work and personal life without giving in to failure in either. Her work was coming along just fine, thankfully. She managed to accomplish two of her smaller goals since being sworn into office

and was optimistic about the rest of her term. She still consulted with Sheldon when she needed guidance.

Navigating the muddled waters of her relationship with Pam was a chore but Terrence and Frank helped smooth the bumps along the way. They maintained a supportive friendship circle for one another that helped them all get through the rough times in love and life. Terrence was always a little envious of Frank's bond with Brianna but never let it show. He eventually met a man while volunteering at a shelter that provided food and a night's rest for the working poor and homeless. Frank remained single, exploring his sexuality in the privacy of his home and through online chatting. Yesenia kept her word and remained quiet about her affair with him and Brianna stayed ignorant of the fact. She gave Yesenia a glowing letter of reference to take with her to her next endeavor and was saved the further heartache of knowing that Yesenia and Frank had violated her trust.

Though Brianna found comfort in her friends, she decided that she needed to go home for a few days. She needed some time away and decided to take a weekend to visit her mother and grandmother in New York. The closer she got to the Holland tunnel, the better she felt. She couldn't wait to feel the consolation her family could give. She had told them about everything and they were looking forward to her arrival. Brianna felt a calmness drape over her as she drove. For the first time in a long time, she actually felt relaxed. She was in control.

Losing Control

End

Acknowledgements

To my wife, I give my most sincere and heartfelt appreciation for your patience, your encouragement and your assistance. I love you and continue to be grateful for each day that I wake up with you by my side.

There are many people who have helped me bring this book to life. Some assisted with constructive criticism while the simple encouragement and friendship from others kept me going when completing the story felt like a chore. My mother and my sisters and brothers (in-laws included) and my niece, Jessica Suarez, I thank you for your support. To my "SC" family, you know who you are, thank you. Lynne Womble, Renair Amin, and Marcinho Savant I'm grateful for your friendship. Dava Guerin, my publicist, thank you for all of your hard work. I appreciate and love working with you more than you know. Dr. Michelle Hutchinson, my editorial consultant, thank you so much for helping me polish my work and making it the best it can be for my readers. I enjoy working with you.

Inspiration comes in many forms and from many places, but there are a few people whose presence and or art inspired me and even helped me write certain scenes in this book. Saunders Sermons, we've been friends for as long as I can remember and you still inspire me. Jesse Boykins III and Kuku, your music played a vital role in my writing of certain scenes. Thank you for your talent and sharing your gift.

Biography

Born in Toronto, raised in Miami and now living in southern New Jersey, Cheril N. Clarke is the author of five novels, *Foundations: A Novel of New Beginnings* (2001), *Different Trees from the Same Root* (2003), *Intimate Chaos* (2005), *Tainted Destiny* (2006), *Losing Control* (2009) and one play, *Intimate Chaos*. She has been featured in *Curve* Magazine, the nation's best selling lesbian magazine, *The Princeton Packet*, *Philadelphia Gay News* (PGN), About.com, *Out IN Jersey*, EURweb, *Burlington County Times*, Phillyburbs.com, *Clik Magazine*, Sistah2Sistah online magazine., 247gay.com, Femmenoinre.net, as well as *Crain's New York Business* newspaper, among others. Her editorial work has appeared in *About Magazine*, GayWired.com and on 247gay.com and her opinion columns have been featured by the National Black Justice Coalition.

Clarke was a keynote speaker at an African Asian Latina Lesbians United conference and has performed at events organized by African American Lesbians United for Societal Change. She is simultaneously working on a new script, Asylum, in addition to researching for her sixth novel. She is also getting ready for the Philadelphia production of *Intimate Chaos* the play (May 2009).